Shoot the Messenger

Gregory John Ferris

By the same author

Zoe: An Act In Two Plays

One Hundred and Sixty-four buttons

Inutile

Covid Confinement, Or Much Ado About Muffin

La Famille Bilingue and A Simply Missing

La Petite Maison Du Chocolat

Rendez Vous

To Cristina Martin

CHAPTER ONE

Jason was certain that he was going to regret this trip in the same way that he regretted most everything that had happened in his twenty-eight years.

A few of those misadventures, he admitted silently, had been his own fault. Still, someone could have warned him. They shared responsibility for the consequences, the majority of which, while not catastrophic, were not boast worthy.

"It takes a village" applied to everyone, himself included. Didn't it?"

Regret.

Jason noticed lately that he had begun regretting decisions in advance of making them. Maybe that was a version of progress.

"Is that wisdom?" he asked, instantly regretting those three words intended for a private audience, for they had been uttered aloud.

"What about wisdom?" came a female voice from the rear of the white van.

"A street name?" the same voice prompted.

"This one says Sage." the feminine voice added, trying to be helpful.

"Never mind, Cheville," Jason replied.

"I see it. This is the turn."

He swiveled the steering wheel slightly to the left, passed several houses, then turned the wheels to the right pulling into the driveway alongside a nondescript brick house.

"It's cute," Cheville stated, the words rendered as a final verdict, without possibility of appeal.

"Yes," he agreed pleasantly, adding silently this time,

"I'm going to regret this trip."

Jason's mind flashed back to five days ago.

He had not seen his aunt in several years, and their phone conversations had been nearly as infrequent. So, her call to him, while not a total surprise, had been unexpected.

"A trip," she had said. Whether the word had been meant as a reward or a punishment had been unclear. He knew his aunt well enough to know that she would explain everything to him, in her own time and after her own fashion. Although the explanation itself might be completely untrue, its sole veracity residing entirely within the confines of her head. Sybil was like a semi-drunk that one encounters in bars, one whose story was detailed enough to be plausible, but ultimately as prone to evaporation as liquor itself. Sybil would have made an excellent politician, or minister, or any profession that required a mixture of delusion and lies.

"A short, long trip. As opposed to a long, short trip."

"What does that mean, Aunt Sybil?"

It was to be a road trip then, Jason speculated, and not an air flight, which would have made it a long, short trip. Or so he assumed. Correctly, as it turned out.

2

Sybil proceeded to describe an ambiguous journey. It was to be of indeterminate duration and with no particular destination, other than it would be off the beaten track and, for a peculiar but undisclosed reason, in any direction other than East. In brief, it was a trip, details to follow.

Jason smiled at his aunt's phrase, 'off the beaten track'. Sybil herself lived in the hamlet or village, or town of Brentville, itself off the beaten track in North Central Pennsylvania. She was between the crowded reality of the New England states and the possibilities that sprouted each year in the west. Perhaps that was the origin of her animus against East for this trip. His aunt had lived in Brentville forever, in the same ordinary house that he had visited a handful of times, but which, he would be informed a few days later, was 'cute.'

Jason was perturbed that he had no reason to decline his aunt's command, disguised as it was in such a tempting offer.

He had no job, no family, well that was a half-truth, no pressing engagements, no option to tell Sybil no.

"It won't cost you anything," she assured him.

Sybil would furnish the transportation and provide the majority of provisions, a euphemism for the money that he lacked.

She had adroitly cut his last means of escape.

Two days later, having bummed a ride to Brentville, he stood in the level driveway, regarding the list of chores that Sybil has passed to him, before uttering a word.

"Hello Jason."

3

She wasted no time on small talk.

"It's a simple list."

It was indeed. It contained two items, the minimum to constitute a list.

He read it aloud.

"Have van checked."

"Get gas."

Sybil nodded, then added,

"Regular gas. That high test is a scam, and the cheap stuff is garbage."

"Have the garage bill me," she said, then passed him a $50 bill.

"For gas. Regular gas," she repeated.

"Use any extra for your own maintenance and checkup."

Jason took the proffered money, any hesitation on his part would have only magnified his embarrassment.

"The keys are in the ignition," pointing to single vehicle in the driveway.

"Thanks for pointing it out for me, Aunt Sybil. I might have missed it. It's not exactly eye-catching."

Sybil knew her nephew well enough to verify that Jason had a valid driver's license, while Jason knew his aunt well enough to have obtained one, an excellent counterfeit. They smiled at one another, each pleased with having outfoxed their close relative.

The white Odyssey destined to serve as their transportation was the epitome of conventionality, and the nightmare of vehicles for a young American

4

male. Jason took comfort in the disguise that his ball cap and sunglasses provided. And that they would be 'off the beaten track.' Even juiced with premium fuel, it would remain a big, white box. As for Sybil, she loved the van.

She loved it despite the rarity with which she drove it, her ardor in inverse proportion to the miles that she added to its odometer.

Sybil turned toward the house. He was dismissed, the transaction concluded.

"How long have you owned? Didn't you used to drive a Camry?"

His aunt swiveled slowly back to face him.

"I still do. The Honda is more of collector's item."

"It is? An Odyssey?"

"For me it is. It has sentimental value."

Jason considered his aunt's claim. As far as he knew, she possessed not a gram of sentimentality. If she believed what she had said, the vehicle must truly be unique. He was intrigued.

"Where did you find it?" he asked.

"I bought it about a year ago. From Cassie."

The name was unfamiliar to Jason. He knew no one in Brentville other than his aunt. Apart their infrequent phone calls, Sybil had her world, and he his. That seemed to be fine with her. It definitely was for him.

"Is Cassie a friend?"

She considered his question.

"Part of my entourage is more accurate."

The response was delivered without a hint of jest.

Jason nodded knowingly while wondering if he himself belonged to that non-exalted contingent.

"Probably not," he admitted silently. "A poor relative and a chauffeur to boot."

His aunt's dismissive attitude and sparse words nearly caused Jason to change his mind on the spot. He convinced himself to continue with the upcoming adventure only when he realized that Sybil had asked him, and not this unknown Cassie, to accompany her. That was important, wasn't it? It provided small consolation, but it soothed his ego.

Moreover, Jason had no ride back home. And no money once he got there.

She sensed his discomfort, and overcompensated, talking excitedly about the van.

"It is in fantastic condition, almost new in fact. Cassie sold me the Odyssey after last year's events here in Brentville. You know, with the Smith woman.

Another name unknown to Jason, this one suitably anonymous. His blank look caused Sybil to blush in a combination of anger, and embarrassment that one of the recent highlights in her life was apparently unknown to her nephew, and therefore likely equally inconsequential in the eyes of the general public.

"Oh well, it was big happenings here in town. You can look it up sometime."

Jason made a mental note to not do any research on the history of unknown persons, particularly one with only a first name, probably a nickname and the other, last name only, called Smith, in a tiny, unimportant village.

He chuckled to himself.

"And off the track is yet to come."

Having won the first set, the nephew went to hop dramatically in the van and speed off, but his flamboyant departure was thwarted by having to move the driver's slowly rearward using the control on the door and then rolling gingerly over the speed bump that sat almost exactly in front of the house. He'd have been correct in guessing that it had only recently been installed at his aunt's prodding of Brentville's head of public works.

Sybil watched the van until it disappeared from sight.

She frowned.

Sybil flaunted the van locally as a sort of mobile if cursed trophy, a reminder of the Faulor tragedy. And of the vanquishing of the Smith woman, her latest nemesis. And yet Jason knew nothing of it. It was indeed time for a trip away from her beloved Brentville.

CHAPTER TWO

Monday, Jason had taken the celebrity van to be inspected and readied for the upcoming trip.

The service manager at the Honda dealership and he had spoken at length about Sybil's planned excursion. The majority of the conversation consisted of the mechanic's advice to sell the car somewhere far away and to return to Brentville by any other means.

"The car was cursed," he whispered after looking around to assure that he was not overheard.

"It may still be cursed," the 21st century technician advised Jason.

"Hondas have a reputation for reliability."

"They are reliable. Very reliable. So is this one. But so is a mean drunk. This vehicle brings bad luck"

"Can you order a replacement good luck part?" he had queried, amusedly discounting the repairman's advice."

"I would if I could...Jason" the service manager added, glancing at the paperwork on his clipboard.

"Ask your aunt about this van sometime and see if you don't agree. Sell it along the way."

"And hope that it doesn't follow us home?"

Jason noticed that his flippancy was not appreciated by the older man. Yet Jason was

9

impatient to start this voyage to parts unknown, and he had no desire to delve into local folklore.

"I don't know which direction we are headed, how long the trip will last. She hasn't even informed me of our destination."

"It must be nice for you to just take off on a trip like that. You have to be single. I remember those days vaguely.

Jason nodded.

"Nothing except our departure date. This whole," he paused, before settling for "adventure is one big mystery to me."

It was the manager's turn to nod his head.

"Then maybe this van is the perfect mode of transport for your trip, after all."

"It's her pride and joy, Jason said, steering the conversation to closure.

"She won't sell it. Unless it breaks down along the route."

The manager ignored the unintended slight. Instead, he replied,

"I know all about Sybil's pride, but I've never seen her joy."

"Good luck," were the manager's parting words ninety minutes later as he handed the keys back to Jason.

"Good luck," Jason repeated aloud as he returned to the present. He pulled into the driveway of Sybil's property. He sat there silently, relishing a few moments of peace before venturing to fetch his aunt who stood lit by bright sunlight in front of her cute home.

10

Neither of the two passengers sitting in the rear of the vehicle said a word.

It was time. He exited the Odyssey and walked the dozen paces to where his aunt stood.

"Who are they?" Sybil demanded, her pale blue eyes staring directly into Jason's. There was no need to indicate who, either by pointing or a simple motion of her head.

"You remember Cheville."

"My girlfriend," he added when Sybil shook her head.

"I thought you were seeing someone with a normal name."

"And the boy is named Caleb."

"Her son? What is he doing here? What are they doing here?"

"They are going along."

"Along?"

"They are accompanying us."

"To where?"

"On our trip, wherever that is."

Jason flashed his most charming twenty-eight-year-old smile.

"Where are we going anyway? No time for secrets."

Sybil harrumphed at his nephew's naiveté.

"You'll have to tell me where we are going. Up to this point, you haven't shared much about our destination."

Sybil visibly relaxed from the shock of the unexpected presence of Cheville and the boy. She had transitioned to problem solving mode. At least the boy had a normal, if old fashioned name. A Brentville sort of name she thought idly.

"It's not decided yet."

"Oh" Jason replied, unable to think of anything else.

"You invited them along?"

Jason nodded.

"So, you will just have to disinvite them."

"I can't go if they stay."

"Why not?"

"I have my reasons. Just like you have your reasons"

The sun continued its ascent, searching a better view of the family dispute.

"Cheville and Caleb took the bus from Kittaning, and stayed last night at the Barnier house, just so they would not be late."

"Party crashers are never on time," she wanted to say.

"They could stay there today," Sybil said, knowing that the bus did not run daily.

"It runs weekly. Cheville does not have money for another night, let alone another week."

"Nor do you," Sybil reasoned silently.

"They could stay at your house until we return. When is that?"

"Or we could drop them back in Kittanning."

"We can't. They were staying with friends."

"And now they want to stay with strangers."

"Want has nothing to do with it."

Jason looked around, spotting the roofs and steeples of churches towering in the near distant over the trees.

The sun had attained the perfect vantage point.

"I'd forgotten how many churches there are in Brentville. They could seek refuge in one of those. I guess we have a solution for you after all."

"The purpose of my road trip is to escape temporarily and to learn permanently something of importance. Along the way, have fun. For the two of us."

"That presupposes that we actually begin the trip. We, us, not just you and me. You see yourself as the star in this late in life biopic. We are not simply colorful characters in your movie. They are real people."

"I agree."

"You do?"

"You aren't colorful. Don't be shocked. I didn't select your extras. It was you who cast them into this...what did you call it?""

"A mature biopic," he said boldly.

The two relatives stood there, measuring each other in the quiet of the early summer day, the silence interrupted only by the intermittent sound of the cooling exhaust of the Odyssey at rest, and the chant of songbirds at work.

"So, are they coming with us?"

Sybil paused, very tempted to say no. She regarded him for a long time, judging her nephew's resolve. She wanted to stamp her foot to demonstrate her anger but worried about snapping a heel on her new shoes.

She would find a way to show her displeasure later.

Sybil sighed and said simply, "Let's go."

CHAPTER THREE

Sybil had learned decades before that her best plans usually went awry in some unforeseen way. Typically it was later, and not immediately, as this endeavor appeared to be heading.

She was constantly annoyed at someone or something. It was who she was. Sybil had come to terms with it, although that self-compromise itself annoyed her as well.

The older woman barely glanced at the occupants in the rear as she settled onto the front passenger seat. The younger woman's face was unfamiliar.

"Hi Sybil," Cheville said pleasantly while Jason put the final piece of luggage into the back of the Odyssey.

"I want to thank you for inviting us along on this adventure. You are very kind."

The statement confirmed what Sybil suspected. She would have canceled the trip then and there, but Cheville's use of the word adventure and the imagery it painted, prevented her from exiting the vehicle. She almost reconsidered however, when, as she reclined the seat a few degrees, a moderately high pitched voiced asked,

"Where are we going?"

Sybil shrugged, then realizing that the boy, yes it was a boy she remembered, could not see her response, replied,

"Elsewhere, Caleb."

Sybil's mind flashed back to her early days as a teacher, and the first time that she had shrugged in response to one of her young male student's question.

A shrug was a boy's magic answer, and turning it back on a recalcitrant pupil had been among her most effective tools.

"Where's that?" the boy pursued.

"Somewhere else", Jason replied as he buckled his seat belt.

"Does it matter?" Sybil asked the boy in return.

Sybil pictured the boy's lips contorting to form a response to this serious question from an adult, a stranger at that. She had taught so many boys throughout her career, that now, each new one she encountered seemed to have the combined qualities of all his precedents.

"Strange that she did not experience that same sense of amalgamation with men," Sybil had wondered on several occasions.

Caleb's lips finally arranged themselves and answered,

"I think so."

He launched another question from the rear.

"Which road do we take?"

"This one," Sybil answered, her reply a command to Jason.

The freeway is the other direction," her nephew advised.

"Good for it."

"Head westerly," Sybil said a moment later.

"West would be better," Jason reflected. West was the best word in American English. Westerly was ok, but not great. West was a hastily splashed acrylic that combined speed, simplicity, confidence, optimism. Westerly was the watered-down version, a diet America.

"Are we going to California? Mount Rushmore, Florida, oops, that is South. National parks? Like Yellowstone?" Jason asked.

"Maybe as far as Ohio," Sybil said in a calm voice.

"Ohio?" Caleb asked excitedly, echoed by Jason.

"Ohio where?"

"What?" Sybil replied.

"Which state is Ohio in?"

"Denver," Caleb began.

"Is there an Ohio province in Canada? That would be north."

"Denver is in Ohio," Caleb completed the phrase.

"One question at a time, boys."

"If it is, you have me driving the long way, through Canada to California. It must be out west. Ohio Colorado. Ok, I was confused for a minute."

"Denver is buried in Ohio."

"What?" asked Jason.

"The man who the city of Denver is named after, well his name was Denver."

"Duh."

"He is buried in Ohio."

"Why?"

"Well, they normally bury dead people."

"What is there to see in Ohio, Colorado? Other than this dead man named Denver."

Sybil raised her arms for silence.

"Ohio the state. We may end up in Ohio."

"Tonight? That is not far, Aunt Sybil. And then tomorrow?"

"Just drive."

Sybil had Jason remain on country roads, which, one interstate slash excluded, comprised the entirety of the system that surrounded Brentville.

She soon directed Jason towards the north, not the west that he so anticipated.

It was miles of forest, one great woodland sliced here and there by small farms and even smaller villages.

It was a clear day and they soon climbed to the height of the undulating plateau. A series of ridges characterized the topology, a pattern that resembled large ocean waves stretching to the horizon.

In the distance, a car descended a steep road, visible as flashes of reflected sunlight as it traversed openings in the foliage. It was a silver plumed tropical bird that soon disappeared from sight.

A few hours later, they reached Whitland, a small semi-industrial town set among treed hills. They were 20 miles from New York State, when they stopped. Signs confirmed its nearness, but it was not the New York of Caleb's surprised squeal.

"The city is hundreds of miles and dozens of Starbucks away," Cheville told the excited boy.

"Oh."

18

"Starbucks!" Sybil snorted.

"I've been to one, twice. The second time it was clear there would be no thrice."

"They threw you out?" Caleb asked.

"Was that sincerity, or a child's sneer?" Sybil wondered. She hoped it was the latter. He would be a clever competitor.

Jason said nothing, content to let his aunt's complaint unwind at her pace. He didn't relish her story telling, but so far, she had not corrected his driving.

"What's wrong with Starbucks?" Cheville asked to fill the dead air.

"If I want to attend a costume party hosted by carnies, I will wait until late evening and find one with alcohol."

"The Saint Louis arch," Caleb exclaimed, pointing to a small monument alongside the road.

"It's a scale model, Caleb. The original was fabricated in this area and erected in Saint Louis. Gateways are everywhere, you only need to look for them. "

"Pull in here," Sybil commanded her nephew, having decided to not pack please for this trip.

"A cemetery?"

"It is for a quick visit. It is a good luck charm."

"If you say so."

"It's a local tradition."

"You aren't a local."

"The tradition has spread like Christmas. When you visit here, you're a local. I am today. Don't worry, we aren't staying."

"I wasn't worried about myself."

"It's only for a few minutes. I'm not dead yet."

Sybil marched off and they followed along closely, Caleb at her side like a small tourist intent on hearing every word.

"Do you believe in Christmas?" the child asked

"Of course, dear," she replied with a smile.

The child returned the smile, and then, spotting what he decided must be their goal, ran ahead in order to be first.

"Do you?"

"Do I what?"

"Believe in Christmas."

"No. Of course not."

"Then why..."

"Then why did I tell your son, that I did?"

She did not wait for Cheville's answer.

"Because that is what adults do. We lie to children. That is our role."

"No, it isn't."

"It's kinder? It's our duty? It's our punishment? Take your pick, an answer must be among them somewhere."

Sybil led them to a small marker, one decorated with a bizarre assortment of what could have been kindly termed 'gifts'.

Cheville was the first to notice the oddity.

"A tombstone without a name? Is that legal?"

"They come that way. It has a name, only the dates are missing."

"Yes, you're right. I see that now. Still, is that legal?"

"I suppose that they could get a warrant for his arrest, but to what purpose? He has already reached his end.

Visitors who want to find it have no problem with absent dates."

"Is it a shrine?"

"He would have hated that term, but would have enjoyed the attention, if not the companionship. The modest are the vainest."

"They hide it well."

"They do indeed."

"He was unassuming in life and death," Sybil announced, looking around at the modest grounds

"This is the only good grave on the grounds, no offense to the other deadies."

"You knew him?"

"A long time ago. He helped me."

"How?"

Sybil ignored questions that she did not like, Cheville had perceived that in the short time they had spent together.

"He didn't survive his money, but his investments have done well."

"He has many visitors," Cheville said simply.

"He still has toys," Caleb stated perplexedly.

"Those are gifts. Interest on his investments you might say."

Her mood lightened despite the surroundings.

"He sowed his best efforts among the talented whom he met: artists of all sorts, musicians, comedians, actors, even aspiring businessman, and women. That was unheard of at the time, supporting businesswomen. He asked for nothing in return except a visit now and again to his tomb to some, wherever that would be, and if convenient, a joke, a story, a brief performance at his funeral, whenever that would be.

Needless to say, his funeral was the event of his and others' lifetime

It was the longest and most entertaining service I ever attended. I wasn't the first to joke that he should die every year. And it took off from there."

"The party seems to still be in full swing."

"His grave continues to attract the grateful and the hopeful. Its lucky."

Caleb was fidgeting among this adult conversation.

"Are you going to kiss it?", Jason asked, genuinely curious.

Caleb paused mid-fidget, frozen as if he were one of the sculpted stone angels that this graveyard lacked.

"No," Sybil replied curtly, the brevity of the answer underscoring the silliness with which she considered the question.

Caleb thawed and moved slightly, the disappointment nearly shimmering like melting ice.

"I mean yes," Sybil exclaimed suddenly, refreezing the young boy.

She moved slowly, ritually, to the magic stone, clear a small space among the other offerings, and bending slightly, kissed it ceremoniously.

Caleb's awe was compensation for the foolishness that she herself felt.

"Traditions have to begin somewhere," she said to cover her embarrassment.

"What about us?" Caleb demanded.

The three adults regarded one another.

"Let's play kickball," Jason said suddenly.

"With what?"

"Here?" Sybil asked, surprised but not angry.

"I brought a ball just in case."

"In case of what?"

"If Caleb's toy broke."

"It is not a toy," Caleb protested. "Those are toys," he added, indicating the random assortment of objects that surrounded and nearly covered the tomb of the bringer of luck.

"Or there was no reception, or the charging cable was lost. It's important to have a backup toy," he added," with a wink to Caleb.

"It's Aunt Sybil's gift," Jason said, with another wink, this one for Sybil.

Caleb glanced quickly at Cheville for approval, who nodded.

"Thanks, Aunt Sybil."

"Come on, Caleb, I'll race you to the Odyssey."

The boys ran to fetch their play toy.

"You must enjoy seeing your son run. So many children today are half electronic."

"Caleb isn't."

23

Sybil was not ready to be interrupted.

"I wasn't sure that his legs functioned as dexterously as his overused thumbs. His muscles and ligaments appear to be in working order.

I hope you don't mind me telling him about Christmas. It.."

Cheville interrupted anyway.

"You don't strike me as someone who believes in Santa Claus."

"I don't.

"It isn't a strangers role to.."

"You don't believe in Santa, but you come here to this lucky charm. Sorry. To this place."

"There is a difference. Luck is empirical."

"It's what?"

"It exists."

"I'm sorry. I didn't mean to insult you. I can see that this man was important to you."

"Don't overestimate me, Cheville. He was a good man, rare but not unique. I'm not being maudlin. He had that je ne sais quoi. He was a special person. I'm not being maudlin."

"OK."

"I came here for equal parts respect and what I guess is superstition. Have you noticed that good fortune is distributed randomly, in clumps? It's not like air. You can breathe anywhere."

She demonstrated by taking a deep breath.

"In a cemetery as easily as in a maternity ward."

She watched Jason and Caleb as they reached the van.

"Luck is different. It doesn't come to you, to most of us, unbidden. You have to search it out, like ginseng.

"Is this pilgrimage intended to counteract the bad karma of the van?"

"What are you talking about? Who told you the van has bad karma?"

"Jason mentioned that the mechanic at the garage talked about it. He sounded quite sincere, Jason said. Something about it being haunted."

"That is the most ridiculous statement I've heard in the past year. It's a van, like millions on the road. Bad luck doesn't exist, only good luck."

"That makes no sense, Sybil.

"Maybe not."

"I know about luck. Jason has had bad luck ever since he met.."

"Since you two met? It's nothing to do with you."

"I was going to say that."

Again, Sybil interrupted her.

"It doesn't matter. We all have problems.

"I stopped here to have a new beginning. That is the purpose of a road trip. You may need whatever luck this man may bring us. Jason too. With the four of us, we may get a family sized bucket of good fortune."

"Cross my fingers," Cheville said with a wan smile.

"But for now, I am finished with dead men and their histories."

Caleb returned, his smile proof that his facial muscles were in condition as well.

25

"We can bounce off the tombstones for extra points," Caleb suggested, demonstrating his technique and shouting for the benefit of fans above and below ground, "One nothing," and creating a lively new variation of a child's game in the place where no one ever grew any older.

CHAPTER FOUR

After the cemetery tournament, Sybil had Jason drive them a few miles, before directing him to pull into the parking lot of a Hampton Inn.

"What's wrong? Why are we stopping? Are you sick? Do you have any nausea? We should have stuck to freeways where hospitals are easy to find."

"I saw one a mile back," Cheville added.

"That was a former mental hospital," corrected Sybil.

"Oh."

"It might be worth a visit. Maybe they can help you."

"Is that supposed to be a joke?"

"They have nurses."

"It's been closed for years."

"How do you feel?"

"I feel fine, physically and mentally."

"Lunch?" Caleb asked, unperturbed by adult concerns.

"I'm fine," Sybil insisted

"It is too late for a second lunch," Cheville answered Caleb.

"And too early for dinner."

"Potty break?" Jason suggested.

"We are old enough to drop that phrase, and to speak as adults. Is that alright with you Caleb?" Sybil asked rhetorically.

"OK," the boy replied automatically, not
having listened to the conversation, his mind
distracted by his stomach.

"It's a hotel," Sybil said sarcastically.

"The mental hospital is now a hotel?"

"Are we staying in a hotel?" Caleb asked.

"I'm not staying in a mental institution that is
now a hotel."

"Forget the mental institution, Jason."

"Why do we stop every twenty miles? So far,
we've visited a cemetery full of strangers, and now an
empty hotel. What's next, the abandoned mental
hospital, which may not be a hotel?"

"It's closed."

"So much the better."

"But this hotel is new, and it is open. As it is
probably not empty judging by the cars around us."

Jason paused to gather his thoughts.

"Aunt Sybil, we've only driven sixty miles.
Are you sure you want to stop for the night? It's still
bright daylight. Why?"

"Because I don't want to lollygag."

"What?"

"I'm in a hurry."

Cheville regarded Sybil incredulously. Was
the older woman serious?

"I'm not complaining. This is just an
observation Sybil, but your definition of a hurry
seems to differ than most people. This isn't exactly
the Pony Express."

"If I wanted to work for FedEx or if I were
pressed for anyone else's time, I'd have never left
Brentville. I'm doing this for myself."

"As always," Jason said softly, while Cheville struggled and failed to make sense of Sybil's comment.

"Why do you think I'm rushing us along. This is fast for me. Let's check in."

"The hotel is nearly booked, ma'am."

"Really?"

"Yes, but we do have two rooms available."

"See Cheville, our earlier stop is already paying dividends. Lucky us."

"I haven't heard of a dead tour guide before. It must be a niche market."

"Not three rooms?" Jason asked the receptionist.

While the receptionist rechecked, Sybil commented,

"I'm not paying for a separate room for Caleb, just so you and your girlfriend can play hotel. A moment ago, you were baby talking potty break, and now you've flipped to randy Andy."

Seeing that Caleb was studiously browsing the kiosk of pamphlets describing local attractions, Sybil continued.

"Caleb for one has his mind on the trip. But then he isn't a mature man."

Jason opened his mouth to speak, but whatever response he had prepared was mooted by the confirmation that only two rooms were available.

"I'm surprised that the hotel is so full," Jason contented himself with saying.

"We are the only full-service hotel for miles. The next nearest one is over the border."

She said border as if crossing it was hazardous, distant, and demanding of a visa.

"This is fine," Cheville said, the words spoken in an odd bi-tonal voice that was at once a statement to the clerk, and a question for Sybil.

"Is there a porter for our luggage?"

"We have carts over there. The one with the duct tape, has a stuck wheel, so you probably want to use the other."

"Restaurant?"

"There is an Applebee's a quarter of a mile down the road. It can be a nice walk if you don't mind the tall grass. But they have loads of parking."

"Room service?"

"You can order pizza delivery."

"Door dash?" Caleb asked, anxious to join in this new game.

"What's that?" the clerk asked.

"Yes, what is that?" Sybil asked.

"I don't know. One of the rich kids at school said he used door dash in a hotel on vacation."

"That reminds me," the young woman behind the counter said, raising Sybil's hopes.

"Yes?" she asked expectantly?

"Housekeeping is only once every four days, if you decide to extend your stay. The hotel has a great deal to offer."

"I can see that," Sybil replied.

"Sorry about the housekeeping, really I am. Covid, you know."

As the acronym celebrated its first birthday, it had become a nationwide mantra and excuse.

"It is the American equivalent of 'God willing'," one of Brentville's clever residents had advised her. It had become tiresome.

Sybil joked, in order to banish Covid from her mind,
"I have my own housekeeping technique. I decorate with dust; it's my signature touch."
"Why are you so busy?" Jason asked.
"We are the county seat, and we are also pretty industrial. We have attorneys, and engineers, construction guys."
"Any young, good-looking ones?" Sybil inquired.
The clerk laughed at Sybil's quip, then blushed when she realized that the older woman was serious and awaiting a reply.
"You would notice men," Sybil prompted, pointedly glancing at the clerk's unadorned left hand.
"A few," she replied.
"Some salty hunks your age as well," she added, her face blushing anew.

Once installed in their room, with Caleb in the bath and safely out of earshot, Cheville had harsh words for Jason.
"I didn't believe what little you've told me of your aunt. I took it for small town gossip, or your mother's jealousy.
Sybil is a one-woman sexcaspade, and you volunteered to be her roadie. I can't imagine why she invited us along."
"You're imagining things, Cheville."

"I need a shower to wash off her grime. You or Caleb can have the bed near the window. The other the floor. The carpet looks four day clean."

CHAPTER FIVE

The four travelers met in the lobby and drove the short distance to dinner.

"I can catch a ride back or walk if you three tire out early."

Cheville elbowed Jason as a way to reiterate the point she had made in their room earlier.

Despite the receptionist's optimism, the Applebee's was strangely bereft of both available or desperate men.

"It's been overhunted," Sybil said to herself.

The menu too offered little selection.

"The COVID signs are disappearing, but advertisements for great food specials are not replacing them. They will be collectors' items in two decades."

"Do you really think so?"

"Probably."

Cheville predicted,

"They will be hung on the walls of Cracker Barrel restaurants as inexpensive, harmless nostalgia. Like ads for tobacco."

"Oh, what joyful news is that. I'll be in one of those fields," Sybil said, pointing idly out the window. It was clear that she was irritated.

"There is a distinct absence of male diners," Cheville said nonchalantly.

"In a deep, warm grave. Dead from starvation in Whitland."

"Graves are usually cold, I think," Cheville corrected.

"The menu looks good," Jason said cheerfully.

"Don't get your hopes up," Sybil admonished. She was still pouting.

"Covid doesn't kill plants, I just don't understand why I can't have all the same things that I did in 2019. *We are out of that, no eta today,*" she sang to the tune of *Dashing Through the Snow.*

The usual pleasantries with a waitress were instead a negotiation. The offers bounced from what they desired, only to be returned with what she had in house

It was a match between non-equals. Their high hopes were refuted by slight, nearly imperceptible shakes of her head, with many references to the deity of low inventory

Wallowing in their misery did not improve their condition, although alcohol sharpened their complaints, but only to each other, as their server had more important chores than attend to them.

"Why are some items absent in Heaven, but here on Earth?" Sybil ventured.

"Gravity?" Caleb suggested.

"Because the wait staff has gone to hell."

The food, such as it was, came and went, and soon the dejected adults trudged to the van, followed by Caleb, who, despite the adult whining, had enjoyed the meal immensely.

CHAPTER SIX

The next day was similar to the preceding. They drove a bit, toured a bit, ate a bit, and found rooms for the night.

"We need two rooms," Jason said hesitantly, his embarrassment evident.

"Of course Jason," Sybil laughed, "we can't all fit in one room. And they've no suites. It's like a house without a kitchen," Sybil answered idly.

"Who would want a house without a kitchen?"

"Most women I know."

"I meant.".

"I understand Jason, you need your privacy. Maybe tomorrow or the day after, Caleb can stay with me"

"Really?" Caleb asked, his youthful voice rising in pitch.

"Really has several interpretations. Let's see how its defined tomorrow."

"I mean.." Jason repeated. But this effort at communication failed as quickly as had its predecessor.

"I'm too old to be a prude, or to pretend to be one. Unless a man wants me to be. A man not my nephew," she added quickly.

"Men tire of prudes, eventually they desire her unwrapped. Oh Jason, don't blush. One would

35

think that you.. oh never mind. Caleb is proof of that."

"Proof of what?"

"Take your key. The room has two beds."

"Is there an extra cot?"

"Does Cheville snore?"

"No, Cheville does not snore," the younger woman pounced.

Sybil faced her nephew, waiting for confirmation.

"No, she doesn't snore."

"I told you I don't snore."

"It's like someone saying that they aren't delusional. How would they know? It's not that I don't believe you."

"Fine. Its settled then. Two beds." Cheville said.

Sybil turned to the assistant manager at the front desk.

"Excuse me, but could you have a cot delivered to room 319, please."

"Certainly."

"Fine. Its settled then. Two beds and a cot."

Sybil confides to the receptionist where her traveling companions had gone.

"You would think that they are my age, and me theirs. They act as if this is the 19th century. And here I believed the younger generations were so tolerant and sophisticated. It's all book sophistication, a charade for folks who live it instead of playing the game. They have slept in their bed, now it's time to make it."

"We do that. Housekeeping does. Oh, that isn't what you meant. I may not be sophisticated either. Sorry."

"I suppose you do, make the beds." She smiled at the flustered receptionist. "If only those two knew how."

Sybil turned and started towards the elevator, pulling her small red wheeled suitcase behind.

"We should stay in hotels all the time," Caleb counseled the adults the next morning, between mouthfuls of the bland but bountiful food available on the hotel's breakfast bar.

"Can we?" he asked.

"For a while we can," Sybil answered, the only one in a position to do so.

"Great. Thanks Aunt Sybil," he replied enthusiastically before rising to make yet another trip to the buffet.

The three piled into the Odyssey, knowing their assigned places. Sybil would join them once she had assured herself that she had not overlooked a prospect in the dining area.

"Another day on planet Sybil."

"I'm sure the planet can handle a Sybil sabbatical," Jason replied

"But can we?" Cheville asked lightly

"The fact that Sybil complains constantly is sufficiently annoying. That she is nearly invariably correct squares the annoyance level.

It isn't the message that is unwelcome, it is instead the messenger."

"I'm the driver and she's the messenger. What does that make you two?" Jason asked in an effort to defuse the tension.

"I'll let you know. Soon."

"No one likes a smart ass, other smart asses included."

"That girl is such a pita," Caleb said quietly as Sybil opened the door and settled in.

Although heard by all, the boy's comment was unanimously ignored.

"If I'd known you were going to be so long, Aunt Sybil, I'd have turned off the ignition. It looks like another hot day. Every little bit helps save the planet."

His statement was a private joke, as he knew that it boxed his aunt between her desire to be frugal and her disdain for climate change theories.

"It's not as if we were just vegetating in Brentville. Carbon footprints disappear quicker if you're moving"

"They do?" asked Caleb.

"Yes. Look up in the sky. Those jets, each one leaving its own trail. Those footprints will be gone in a few minutes. Ours will take a little longer since we're traveling slower than a jet. You'll learn about this later in school."

"I hope not Cheville said quietly.

"I suppose you think that this trip is accelerating the destruction of the planet," Sybil prompted.

Cheville chose to not respond, encouraging to Sybil to pursue another topic. She returned to Caleb's cryptic remark.

"Is that one of your classmates texting you?"

"Yes."

"Some cute pigtailed pita?"

Caleb switched the subject

"Aunt Sybil, if you had a Tesla we could let the car drive itself. We could have stayed in Brentville and done this in VR."

"Virtual reality?" Sybil ventured and was rewarded with a vigorous nod of Caleb's head.

"See Jason, I'm with it."

"Would virtual reality be preferable to the four of us on this road trip?"

There was no response.

"No bumps, no disappointments."

"No stopping for gas, either" Cheville said.

"And no one passing gas either," Jason added, with a sharp look at Caleb.

"It's all the road food and the bumps."

"Well Caleb?" Sybil asked.

"No, it would be terrible."

"You might as well read a book or watch a movie. Or go to sleep and dream of a horse. That would be the fate of a stranger to life."

Sybil paused.

"Would you have preferred that?" Caleb

His head moved from side to side just as adeptly as it did up and down.

"No, this is much better."

"I think so too," Jason said, surprising himself as much as the others.

39

"I bet he gets a planet named after him. Maybe my grandkids will be born on Elon. That would be cool."

"I thought that you weren't going to grow up?" Cheville asked.

"Oh?" said Sybil.

"It's his most recent idea," Cheville explained, air quoting the last word.

"How can you have grandkids if you yourself remain a child?"

"Hmm, I hadn't thought of that."

For a while they drove, crossing over and underneath the same freeway, like a needle trailing thread.

When not rolling along, they passed the bulk of the day attending various local oil and timbering museums.

At one museum, Cheville instructed,

"Don't pout, Caleb."

"Caleb can't find a hat," she said in explanation.

"Take this one," Sybil suggested.

"Great, another advertisement," he declined, replacing the cap on the rack.

He reached for one a few pegs away and tried it on.

"It's blank."

"I can stylo something in later. It will be mine."

They discovered that once, for a short period after the Civil War, the region had supplied ninety percent of the world's oil and provided lumber for innumerable construction projects. The industries continued to provide employment for a minority of the area's residents, but the glory days lay in the past. Several of the museums were installed in magnificent Victorian homes, absent their deceased baron builders, yet the buildings themselves bore testimony to past wealth.

Others were situated in large sheds, whose dirt floors were better suited to hosting the heavy equipment of a bygone era.

Caleb and Jason were fascinated by the old technology and the scope of change over the preceding century.

Yet for someone who had organized the trip and selected the stops, Sybil seemed strangely disinterested in the various exhibits. Her attention was captured momentarily by a few aged photos, but for the most part she people watched.

Caleb noticed.

Cheville planted herself in one of the few padded chairs, or simply stood outside in the sun, enjoying the sense of nothingness.

Caleb noticed that, as well as the museum attendees.

The other visitors were dissimilar to their party, consisting mainly of older men in pairs or threes.

Sybil and Cheville found themselves seated next to each other at what was to be their last stop of the day. The males were enjoying the exhibits, but it was clear that they were tiring.

"Caleb has lasted longer than I expected."

"It must be the novelty."

"Probably. Usually his stomach drives him."

"I'm familiar with the vagaries of male digestive systems. It gives them mood swings. Male menopause that runs in reverse to ours. We can have dinner after this one."

"Museums are like cemeteries. They are places to peacefully purge oneself of history, sometimes even of sentiment and sorrow."

"Is that why you brought us here? Excuse me for saying so, but you don't seem very taken by any of the exhibits."

"Not really. They have other uses. Regardless, everyone is happy to step away. Visitors may have remorse as having left too soon, but none at having left. You find them boring?"

"I find most things boring."

"I am sorry to hear that, Cheville."

"I am sorry to hear myself say it."

"I dream of living in a city."

"You are subjected to hordes of urban worms in cities, small towns can't support many."

"What are those?"

"You must have seen them; they have the emaciated look of a failed extra in a Holocaust movie."

"Druggies?"

"They don't make that type of movie any more though. The world is back to hating Jews, as much as Nazis. It's a strange world we live in. It is safer to avoid."

"I'm doing my best."

"Big cities aren't anyone's best these days."

She returned to her original sore spot.

"Or they could be filming one of those post-apocalyptic movies where zombies roam uncontrolled. It's life imitating art, if you ask me."

"I don't recall anyone doing so."

"There is no refuting that we have an oversupply of skinny, drug, nicotine, and booze addled men and women, all aged beyond their years."

"Addicted to addiction," Cheville observed.

"That sums it up."

"They are offset by millions of the other side of the scale, addicted to food, and baubles that they can stuff, inhale, or inject into their bloated bodies."

"Where does that leave us?"

"You're only left if you choose to be."

The two women sat there silently, then Cheville spoke.

"We are taking back roads. Deliberately."

"That's true."

"This pace is quick for you, but it is so slow for me."

Sybil said nothing, and Cheville hurriedly added,

"It is what I needed. Thank you."

"For providing me the space to think and not have to worry about."

"About what?"

"Everything."

"That is too much to worry over. Take it from me and pack fewer concerns. Its more comfortable for your shoulders and hips."

"That is easy for you to say."

"Because I have less time than you to worry about problems?"

Cheville blushed.

"Let's slow it down even more."

"It?"

"Life."

"Life?"

"Yeah. Yes. Sure. Our life, this dialogue. We can talk." It was a question

Cheville nodded.

"Let's talk. Normally. As if life were normal, as if we agreed, as if we were normal and life was regular, normal, that is, and as if it and you weren't in a rush to plunge into a place you don't want to be."

"Is it that obvious?"

"It's obvious because I know my nephew. I'm sure today's visit has given him some crazy ideas."

"Yes, you know your nephew."

"Did your husband like museums?"

"Which one?"

"Oh, I don't know. This one for example."

"Which husband?"

Cheville blushed but recovered from her embarrassment in realizing that Sybil was inviting questions.

"I was like Goldilocks and the seven dwarfs."

"Isn't that the three bears?"

"My life never followed any recognizable script."

"Was it one of your husband's graves that we visited in Whitland, your first."

"Oh no, that wasn't him."

"Then perhaps we will stop at his grave on this trip."

"That might be nice."

Cheville leaned back contentedly

"Really?"

"Yes, really. If only I could recall where I had him buried."

Cheville jolted back upright.

Sybil explained with further prompting.

"I didn't attend the actual service. Something came up."

"Or someone?" Cheville ventured, the churchlike silence of the museum offering her courage.

"You could say that."

"And your husband not yet cold," Cheville observed, cautious to add no emotion to her words.

The critique required no spice.

"There you are wrong. He'd been cold, frozen really, for years. Where do you think I caught my chill? It was like early covid, the aftereffects seem to endure, whether they are real or imaginary."

"My first husband died from stress. Did Jason tell you?"

"He mentioned only that your husband had died."

"Folks say that I complain. You should have seen him. Be glad that you did not. That may have been my inheritance. Do you think that possible?"

Cheville nodded politely.

"That was the reason I skipped the service. I was afraid, it seems silly now, it seemed silly them. I was afraid that he would criticize the itinerary and food at his own wake from beyond the grave, which itself also displeased him now that he occupied it.

A woman approached them. She was young and blonde, small and lithe, strong. She was powerful enough to carry around a 17-pound child for hours every day of the week, no off days. She explained that she was here with her grandfather, who enjoyed such things.

A few minutes later, the presumed grandfather came to apologize and to take her away.

"We return to cemeteries not in order to raise the dead but to bury our ghosts," Sybil said, resuming the conversation where they had paused it.

"Few of us can have everything, many have nothing."

"And you?"

"I redefined the meaning of something and went for that."

Sybil pointed to the exhibitions that lay before them.

"You need to find your something."

Sybil and Cheville regarded one another and smiled, then looked up to find Jason and Caleb standing in front of them.

"Thanks for bringing us here, Aunt Sybil."

"What did you find interesting?"

"All of the men had one thing in common.

They were willing to risk all for the big chance."

Cheville and Sybil shared a glance while Jason expounded on his discovery.

"Of course, it's all old technology, but once it was brand new. And today we have new ideas and opportunities."

"That is good to hear, I suppose," Sybil said flatly.

"I have an idea myself."

The women remained silent, hoping that their silence would prevent any further explanation. Jason perceived their flat expressions as encouragement.

"Bitcoin is down. Now is the time to buy and ride it upward."

"Where is upward?"

"To the moon."

"Where there is no life."

"No oxygen," Caleb added unhelpfully.

"It's an expression. There is money to be made."

"Have you ever made money? Real money?"

"Its new. Like all this was, once," said Jason, sweeping his hands to indicate the contents of the museum."

"New," he repeated.

"As are the contents of the dumpster behind a restaurant. New garbage remains garbage.

They even sell bitcoin at the ATM, which is stuck in a corner across from the elevator doors in hotels. It's the same location where stood ashtrays long ago. The same value in my opinion.

You can buy Bitcoin at Giant Eagle like one of those crane arcade games that carnivals have to lighten the burden of money from children."

"You are what we call 'risk adverse'."

"There is no we Jason, only you. I say that you are blind to risk. So on balance we are." Sybil trailed off, having lost her train of thought.

An awkward moment followed her pause, during which the two rearmed.

"The center of a seesaw doesn't move," Sybil said finally, instantly regretting how stupid her comment sounded.

Jason laughed mockingly.

"Did you read that in a fortune cookie?"

"As a matter of fact, I did," Sybil admitted, laughing at her own silliness.

"What does it mean."

"Who knows? Other than proving that I've been inside a Chinese restaurant."

"I'm surprised that you ventured into any sort of Chinese establishment. Did you enjoy it?" Cheville asked, in order to end the talk of crypto. None of them were knowledgeable enough to discuss it intelligently.

Sybil looked steadily at her nephew.

Crypto, currency. It was meaningless words overlayed on unrealistic dreams. That was irresistible bait to men of Jason's age. No, not true. At thirty, Jason should have aged out of this childlike optimism and left it behind like a bag of penny candy, no longer sweet to the taste.

"Confine your dreams to waking hours and leave the nightmares to sleep."

"What do you think, Cheville?"

"The world is filled with lies. I find it more pleasant to think of them as dreams and aspirations and imaginings. We don't criticize each other nocturnal dreams, we treat them with respect."

Sybil's gaze shifted to Cheville, grateful for the timeout. She then turned to Caleb and asked,

"Would you like to have Chinese food tonight?" unsure if the boy had experienced cuisine other than last night's Applebee's or fast food.

He nodded vigorously, content with the word food.

As they walked toward the exit, Caleb looked up at Sybil and asked her,

"There are a lot of grandpaps here and in the other museums. Is one of them yours?"

Cheville, suddenly realizing the true purpose of Sybil's itinerary, quipped,

"All of them, take your pick."

CHAPTER SEVEN

Jason and Cheville were enjoying a few moments of Sybilless time in the Hampton's breakfast area. Caleb was on his first trip of the morning to the food bar.

"It's odd that the guy from the Chinese restaurant last night was staying here," Jason said.

"Why would that be strange? There is one hotel. This is the only game in town."

"By the way," Cheville added, "they likely thought the same thing about each other."

"You don't think.."

"I have no doubt that after our return, they went upstairs and feng shiued all night long."

Jason brought his cup of coffee to his lips, frowned, and replaced it untouched on the small table.

"Sybil is out of men in Brentville. And so, she is searching for companionship. Its dating the old-fashioned way. It's her way."

"That is such a sweet way to put it, Jason. I'd say that she is leaving the town lay fallow while she seeks to lay new fellows. And we've only just begun. I wonder if I should keep count to pass the time. It would be fun, like counting blue cars. I'm stuck in the back seat anyway, so what else is there to do? You won't let me drive. On the other hand, you are up there in the front with her, within arms and lips reach."

"I'm safe, as we are too closely related to get any closer."

"Are you sure?"

"Plus, she doesn't like to drive."

"What about me?"

"Sybil is old fashioned that way."

"Oh," was all Cheville replied.

Was that tinged with disappointment, he asked himself.

"I meant as far as me driving."

"I know what you meant."

"You can ride in the back with Caleb. He is yours as much as mine. Does Sybil know that you that you don't have a valid license?"

"We all have secrets. I sometimes wonder if that is why she has us taking these backroads."

"She knows then?"

"I don't think so. I'm driving ok."

"Your driving matches your license."

"Sybil hasn't complained about it."

"She is still on page one of her grievances."

The couple stopped speaking as Caleb returned, each hand holding an overflowing plate, accompanied by Sybil, who was holding a cup of tea, with the string of the sachet hanging limply down the side of the paper cup, and a smaller cup half full of cream in her other hand.

"Good morning, all," Sybil said as way of greeting. She set the cups down, then hung her purse over the back of her chair.

She sat, looked at them in a way that gave the impression that she was offering them a moment to report to her anything of significance. When they said nothing, she turned to watch Caleb eat while her tea steeped.

His dining was not the most pleasing attraction, and she soon focused her attention on Cheville and Jason.

"The Chinese food has given me an idea."

"About men?" Cheville asked.

Sybil thought of ignoring the jab, but she was in a good mood from the previous night.

"No one likes a smart Alec."

"No one likes a smart ass, other smart asses included," Jason echoed.

"Jason, I don't like that sort of talk. I've told you before. It's crude and unrefined."

"She's right, Jason. We can't tolerate crudeness and lack of refinement on this trip. It gets in the way of our," Cheville paused for effect, "evening cultural experiences."

"I speak modern American," Jason said defensively.

"Try a foreign language."

"Yeah, right."

"Yes, right. That is my idea. Thanks to Caleb."

The boy's attention at the mention of his name.

"He must be getting full," Sybil joked, and the other two adults smiled at the truth of her observation.

"Do you remember how you mentioned that Denver is in Ohio?"

Caleb nodded.

"We are going to Colorado after all?" Jason asked, his voice rising.

He raised a hand in preparation of a high five, but lowered it in response to Sybil's command,

"Put your hand down."

"We are not going to Colorado," she said, emphasizing the word not.

"Not foreign language tapes. Don't tell me that we are going to have to listen to foreign language tapes during your musical hour."

They had taken turns in selecting which Sirius/XM station to listen to in the Odyssey. It had been an effective compromise in that all four of them were equally dissatisfied.

"Its strange Jason. We are related and yet you only complain in the morning."

"You don't spend evening with him," Cheville joked.

Jason was not to be deterred.

"Foreign language tapes," he repeated.

"Caleb might be able to take it, but he's young, with a powerful immune system. He can survive your jokes and your 'ideas'".

Sybil nodded. It was an effective way to close a man's mouth.

Jason sat there, awaiting her verbal agreement.

She lifted the bag from the now brewed tea, let it drip for a few seconds, then placed it on one of Caleb's empty plates, pour the entire contents of the cream into the tea, and then lifted the used tea bag and dropped it softly into the space left behind by the cream. She wiped up the remaining tea debris from Caleb's plate with a paper napkin and placed it atop the tea bag. She then set the entire package back on the dirty plate.

"When you have a moment, dear" she gently ordered Caleb.

The boy left and returned quickly, aware that something was about to happen.

"We are going to Lemanche."

CHAPTER EIGHT

The town was unlike any other they had seen. It was part theme park, part cosplay, one hundred percent functional.

One would have thought of a French-Canadian town. It was small, satisfied to remain so, clean, intent on remaining so, a town that had progressed on its own, unique path since it has been forfeited as part of New France after the Seven Years War. The old flag of France flew proudly, if slightly below the Stars and Stripes, a meld as beneficial as that of Lafayette and Washington.

Caleb was astounded at the difference in the town, flabbergasted to find no official website of it online.

"Some of us prefer to live IRL," Sybil said, proud of having learned a word in the language she despised.

"The internet is not life," Cheville added.

"It's full of urban worms."

"Look it up," Sybil suggested. If you can't find it, that doesn't mean that don't exist.

"This town is consolation for having missed Paris."

"When was that?"

"In the past, numbers don't matter there. It's interesting that this town was part of New France.

The British has New England, and the French had their New France.

"When was that?" Caleb asked.

"In the past, where numbers don't matter," teased Jason.

"Weren't you a history teacher?" Cheville inquired.

"In the past" Sybil replied, "you know the refrain."

Lemanche was part artist community, part artisan haven, part immersion language, and food paradise.

"Is this a theme park?"

"I think that it may be what a theme park aspires to be."

It was New Orleans without the flooding, but nearly the same humidity.

The town celebrated two independence days, French and American. Bilingual signs were abundant, but folks get lost in both languages. So there were photos as well, and they are in everyone's native tongue.

It did not require literacy in any language to recognize the long lines and wonderful odors as directions to a bakery.

They were fortunate to find a sidewalk table. Sybil ordered a Kir, Cheville and Jason a beer, and Caleb a limonade, simply because he liked how it sounded in a foreign language. The ate much too much but found time to peruse the shops, but not before Cheville noticed Sybil passing Jason what could only have been an envelope of money.

Sybil stopped in several of the bookstores, a typical meeting place of the community.

The division of a people by age and politics was noticeable on one hand by the absence of books and authors she had read as a child and young adult, now all gone and worse than forgotten by the newer generation. She wondered for a moment if the printers simply hired English majors from India to update the classics that she remembered and marketed them under catchy sounding names of imaginary authors. No, surely someone would catch on, and demand a cut. She told herself to browse the youth section someday soon.

As to the political diatribes, in large print and on harsh paper, they should have been placed in the sports or hate speech racks, both those were overstocked. Still, they sold well.

"Caleb, notice that man over there."

"The one holding the thick book?"

"Yes. The thicker the book, the less it has to say. Words are not meaning, but its search.

Time wasted by the author, the reader, the printer. Years spent by the tree growing the required number of pages. It's all so... wasteful," Sybil preached.

"There are much better uses for limited days."

"Our prime," Caleb interjected, surprising the others with his interest.

"Yes, they do. Men's primes are so short. It is a shame."

"I'm happy to see that you have empathy for my gender and our limitations."

"It's a shame for me, Jason.

"You need someone in his prime."

She laughed at Caleb's directness. She'd have said the same, behaved the same if their roles had been reversed.

"My mother, she used to be in her prime," Caleb said, causing Sybil to wonder what had occurred to change Cheville's attitude so markedly.

Sybil bought two paperbacks in French, and Cheville nudged Jason,

"I bet she reads no more than a few words."

"So what? Maybe she's learning French."

"It's bait."

"Bait? Bait for what?"

"For men of course. That is her entire life."

"Hmmm, would it work for me?" Jason quipped.

Cheville frowned.

"You need something to work for you. Better yet, you need to work for something."

"Caleb, have you seen this three-dimensional popup book on dinosaurs? If I were your age, I'd be all over it."

"If I were 4 years younger, so would I," he replied without a trace of sarcasm.

"Well, I'm buying it anyway," grabbing two candy bars as well.

Back in the odyssey, on their short drive to the hotel, Caleb was loquacious, as if he had drunk a Kir as well.

"You need to get out more often, Aunt Sybil," Caleb counseled.

"I thought that you taught boys my age?"

"Older boys, Caleb. Ones your age still need to be housebroken," Sybil teased.

"You are too old to be a basement dweller."

"What's that," she asked, inadvertently making his point.

"A couch potato," Jason supplied.

"I'm happy to hear that," Sylvia responded, her eyes busy reading the ingredient list on the candy bar.

"What's in it? Cancer stuff?" asked Caleb.

"Caleb!" Cheville scolded.

"Not at all. I wanted to verify that this was full strength, with real sugar and not that saggy stuff that will kill you quicker than COVID."

"I'm not sure that I want to grow older," Caleb volunteered. Maybe I'll stay where I am.

"The rear seat does suit you, Caleb."

"My age I mean."

"So do I. The young ride in back."

"And adults ride up front?"

"Yes."

"By that measure, you should be way up front, clinging to the grill."

Sybil pivoted in her seat. She wanted to slap him, but her shoulder was sore and Celeb too quick. Plus it would concede defeat. Maybe there had been alcohol in Caleb's limonade. Well, nothing could be done about it now.

She laughed instead.

"Perhaps I will on the return trip, like a November deer harvested in hunting season."

The mention of return extinguished the pleasantness in the cabin

"How much longer?" The unspoken words hung in the air like phantoms. No one desired an answer

"But that's not for a while."

Nevertheless, the moment of revelry had passed, the countdown begun, if only subconsciously.

Caleb was the first to recover. He burrowed deeper into his leather covered seat and recommenced his anti-aging theory, and his intent to remain at single digits.

"Adults are unhappy? Why is that? Death?"

The adults shrugged in unison. The body language answer was vague, meaningless in its own way, but it was a spontaneous consensus.

Recognizing the absurdity of the situation, then adults shrugged again in harmony, and then burst into unplanned laughter. Death had passed through, its noticeable absence regifting humor to the van's occupants

"I doubt that you've discovered or will discover eternal youth Caleb, but you've made me feel younger than I have in decades."

"Young enough to switch seats?""

"Sure, at the next stop."

"That's the hotel."

"It's a start."

"What does that window sticker mean?" he asked, disappointed but not deterred from conversation.

"Which one?"

"That one," he replied pointing to a gray Jeep. "It says slut life."

"Sybil can answer your question. She's an expert."

"What?" Sybil demanded

"The window sticker, it reads, oh," Cheville paused, "it says Salt Life. They enjoy going to the beach, honey. Salt air, see?"

"Oh, yeah."

"How was your limonade, Caleb?" Sybil asked.

"It tasted funny."

"I bet it did."

Cheville wanted an early night, and the threesome headed to their room, leaving Sybil to herself.

"I'll manage," she told them, indicating a man standing in the lobby.

"That's Maurice, he's a local. I met him in the bookstore. Maybe he'll take me for a limonade."

Maurice nodded and smiled as the three stepped into their elevator.

Cheville awakened, having thought that she heard a knock on the hotel door. She glanced at the clock on the nightstand, it was 2:12 AM. She listened again; it was silent.

She padded to the restroom and heard the knock again as she finished her business. It was not at their door.

Cheville crept to her door and peaked through the fisheye lens.

63

It was a naked man, Sybil's beau. He
knocked again, and then, either sensing Cheville's
presence or desperate for an alternative, turned and
rapped on her door.

Cheville was hesitant to open the port to a
nude, drunken stranger in the middle of the night.
"Does the time of day really matter all that much,"
her inner voice asked.

"What could she do? Ring Sybil" she told
herself.

Besides he wasn't really a stranger. He was
Jason's aunt's boyfriend. Or something close
enough to merit one call from behind a locked door.

Yes, she would call. But in a minute. She
reached back into the bathroom and retrieved a large
bath towel. One towel, that would suffice. One call
and one towel. Housekeeping was still coviding in
the hotel. The man would understand.

"What's his name?" she asked herself. If she
was going to pass Jason's aunt's nude, drunken
boyfriend one of her precious full size bath towels at
02:14 in a hotel hallway, she should really know his
name. If he wasn't a stranger, then why could she
not recall his name.

She took a deep breath, opened the door a
few inches and handed him the white emergency
coverup.

"I'll call Sybil."

"Who?"

Cheville relegated him to stranger status,
pointed across the hall and said,

"Sybil. That is her room."

"Oh yeah," he said.

"I thought that I was going to the bathroom and must have opened the room door by mistake."

She nodded, leaving his 'Thank you', to bounce off the wood of the closing door.

She called Sybil and thanked goodness when she answered on the third ring.

Disguising her voice as a man, Cheville said,

"We left your room service delivery outside your door. Bye."

Cheville did not bother to see how the late-night opera ended but did notice that there were no more raps at the door.

CHAPTER NINE

By the third day, or was it the fourth, Cheville wondered, she was planning her latest escape, this one a double or triple escape.

She gave little thought as to whether the two of them could manage better without her. She had no doubt that she would flourish without them. As for Sybil, she was....whatever. Sybil was not her concern.

Cheville had never had a successful escape, each previous attempt had led to a less comfortable prison. There was something to be said for inertia. Her plans were daydreams, and despite Sybil's admonition that those were the only sort of dreams worth pursuing, she had found them to be thinly disguised nightmares.

Boredom is as strong a motivator as greed or fear.

"Do you think that if you mix both you fabricate boredom," she asked herself.

Maybe she should try good behavior instead, and this prison of Sybil's which she desired desperately to flee, was better than most.

Sybil was inside the diner, chatting with a man while they waited in the van.

"We can't leave her, lets force her to leave us."

"What good will that do us? We will be stuck in some cute little town with no prospects. And we had that already before we left on this fun trip. Where are we anyway?"

"Does it matter?"

"I suppose not."

Caleb spoke up.

"We are in Lemanche. Haven't you been paying attention?"

The adults regarded each other. Who was the parent, the shared look screamed.

"And Aunt Sybil is super," his youthful certainty preempting any debate.

Jason and Cheville shrugged in unison like distorted images of a carnival mirror.

"I hope this trip never ends. Its school and vacation together."

"Really honey?" Cheville asked.

"Its not too much moving around? You tell me so often that we need to settle down."

"This is different. We can settle later."

Cheville nearly asked him where and when, but that would serve no purpose other than to include him in her worry.

CHAPTER TEN

The next morning was glorious. Three of the travelers were at the indoor pool, but only Caleb was in the water.

"Is Sybil still in her room?"

"You know the routine, Jason. Sybil sleeps in, if she has a.... an adequate man friend. I've noticed that her appetite at breakfast is proxy for his performance.".

Jason said nothing, watching Caleb play in the pool an excuse for his silence.

"You signed us up for Sybil's campaign with less information than a voter has."

"I don't vote."

"It shows. I'm not sure if you're her nephew, her campaign manager or her pimp."

Jason joined the unwanted conversation, keeping his eyes fixed on the sole occupant who was enjoying pool time.

"You are being ridiculous. I'm her nephew. That is all. She is lonely. It's clear she wants companionship."

"Yes, every night. Heaven help Caleb's sensitive eyes if your aunt spots a handsome hitchhiker. She won't wait until the next hotel room to 'welcome her new companion'."

Jason frowned at the image.

"And if it's a rock group with a broken-down car, well she might ask me to join the party."

"She's different, that's all. A bit odd."

"She may be sick," Cheville said, suddenly serious.

"I mean truly ill."

"Let's drop it. It's her life."

He caught the ball thrown to him by Caleb, and tossed it back, wiping his moist hands on his cotton t-shirt.

"Maybe it's a real illness."

"If it is, she's been suffering with it her entire adult life."

"Why do say that? You don't know her. You said so yourself."

"From the little I know and the lot that she has told us."

"The lot that she has told us? That's zero. So, you know nothing, essentially. Your knowledge is the same as mine."

The music was playing, passing uninterrupted over the change of the hour. None of the four were listening. Each of the car's occupants was deep in their own thoughts, daydreams that they considered plausible plans, unique designs that shared a common future, one without any of the other three people in the vehicle. They envisioned the absence of the others as essential, their fellow travelers undesired, ready to be shed of.

Sybil regretted not having embarked alone on her trip. It was her trip, and the driving was not arduous. She could have brought along an electronic assistant, like the one that Caleb used incessantly. Yes, she could have done this alone. Young people were such a burden. Still, they had their uses.

"What are you watching?", Sybil asked
Caleb, who had his eyes fixed on the small rectangle,
while the large screen passed by outside his window.

"Reverend Jim."

"Don't trust men without last names," Sybil
said.

"That is good advice, Caleb. Sybil is an
expert."

"It's such a beautiful day, it almost makes one
believe in a higher power," Jason said.

"The churches are so pretty," Cheville
commented.

"We have a surplus of churches in Brentville.
Most towns do, it's a series of prototypes, one failure
after another."

"As to a higher power, I believe in God every
other day, but trust Him less frequently."

"And the devil?"

"Not at all. He's extraneous. I ask you, what
purpose does he serve? I lie to myself more
convincingly than any being, natural or supernatural,
and I promise myself delicious dreams that are
incredibly plausible."

Cheville questioned whether she should
believe in Caleb. He wasn't her problem, not if she
didn't want it to be hers. She regretted instantly
classifying the boy as a problem, but her guilt did not
resolve the situation. She could not resolve it alone.
So was he worth it, was he worth her belief? As to
Jason, there was no doubt. She owed him nothing.

"I slept well, but not for long. How was your
night?" Sybil asked with a grin.

71

"You must stop reading and believing every trashy item that you can lay your hands on, Aunt Sybil. We aren't all, you know, maniacs, hooking up at the drop of a hat. You may have noticed I don't wear a hat. Neither does Cheville.

"You are wearing one now."

"It's a cap, not a hat. I thought you taught English."

"I like hats. They are fun to drop now and again."

"I need a hat," Caleb volunteered.

"Why do you need a hat?"

Caleb could think of no answer other than because. He said nothing.

"If you told me once, it was long ago, and I don't recall the story. How did you two meet?"

"Through her sister."

"Oh?"

"It didn't last."

"With her sister."

"I see," Sybil said, although she didn't. She could pry again later when she wasn't tired, and he was.

"I think that she was Jason's true love," Cheville said.

"Until he found you, obviously. True loves are replaceable. Otherwise that would be too cruel. Besides, a person has room for a great deal of love."

"Do you think that is true?" asked Cheville.

"We reserve truth to such inhumane places as court, where we demand its presence under threat of punishment from absent gods and armed guards. Truth telling is so against human nature. It's

72

perfectly American. It is far better to teach its lesson in small doses.

"I googled road trips," Caleb said, reentering the conversation.

"Of course you did."

"If there's a kid along, like me, he is usually weird but smart.".

"We settled for you."

"I end up dead, or almost. I mean he does."

"Caleb!" Cheville admonished.

"Death can be funny after the fact, unappreciated at the moment of delivery," Sybil said.

"I have a simple solution," she stated, and waited for the boy's curiosity to peak.

"Google it."

"Google what?"

"To see if you die on my trip. Let me know what you find. That will provide us time for a replacement."

I" can't Google that!"

"Why not? Are you afraid?"

"No! Well, no. I can't search the future."

"Then of what benefit is that contraption?" Caleb laughed.

"Contraption! I like it. It's like a box for crap. Who would want one of those?"

"Indeed."

"Contraption," he repeated.

Cheville spoke up.

"This is our trip."

Sybil raised her eyebrows and regarded the younger woman over glasses that had slid partially down her nose.

"This trip is ours to write. And ours to finish in our own way."

Sybil shrugged slightly as way of acknowledging the correction.

"That is what we all say.

"I hate the internet."

"It might hate you back, Aunt Sybil, give it time."

"There is more to life than electrons."

"Food," said Caleb.

"Family," said Sybil.

""When did you learn that word? It sounds foreign when you pronounce it."

"Strangers, to be blunt, mostly get in the way. Every day, more and more arrive, trampling on your existence. I hope that your son can break his addiction to that device, Cheville" Sybil stated.

"It's an electronic Pandora's box that never empties itself of pestilences.

Doesn't it have some range limitation. How does it work out here?"

"It works everywhere," Caleb said proudly.

"I'm sorry to hear that. I turned off my generation's version of that.... thing," she settled.

"It doesn't seem crowded here," Jason said as they passed one small farm after another.

"Isolate yourself from the billions of opinions of which only a handful are worth considering, and none after you've attained the age of 30."

"They say to keep learning."

"Yeah, one should constantly learn."

"That's crap. People used to die in their late twenties and thirties. Take note of that, you two.

If you haven't learned enough to live by now, you are better off dropping out."

"From life?"

"No, no, no, to life," Sybil said emphatically.

"You're nearing our first stop exit, Jason."

"I am? We've only just started. See," he said, pointing to the odometer with his right thumb, not lifting his hand from the steering wheel.

"You are getting worse and worse, Aunt Sybil."

He regretted his choice of words.

"Besides, I haven't had my radio selection yet."

Sybil ignored his semi-rant.

"You should listen."

"He should?" Cheville asked, as Jason changed the radio station.

Sybil instantly changed it back.

"For a few more years. Especially to me."

A few more years of listening to this woman, Jason asked himself. How long was this trip intended to extend?

"My opinion counts."

"I understand now. There are opinions to ignore, billions in fact, and a few to consider, like you."

"Jason, you're part of this. You are more than just a chauffeur."

"A porter?"

"What will you do if Cheville and Caleb stay here, or in one of the next stops?"

"Carry less luggage? Have a private room? Have you all to myself? Life is good and bad. Don't you always say that?"

75

"I've never claimed any such thing."

"Someone did."

"What will I do?" Cheville's voice continued in a near whisper, but not so quietly that it was not heard in the confines of the cabin.

Her voice resumed its normal volume.

"Yes, what about you, Jason?"

"Today is Wednesday, not pick on Jason day."

"I will keep driving, what else?"

"That's good," Cheville said blandly.

Jason thought no more of the question that his aunt has asked in passing. For Cheville, the words had been monumental.

"Why do you ask, Sybil?" Cheville said.

"I don't really know."

Cheville demurred.

"Is this adequate distance from Brentville?"

"For what?"

"Have we reached a place where you are not only unknown but unheard of?"

"It's near enough to be far enough."

"Your radius is wider than I'd have guessed."

"Has Jason told me about you?"

"No, not really," Cheville answered.

"I don't know you, Sybil."

"You are too young to be forgetful."

"I can't forget what I don't remember. I can't lose nonexistent memories. Sorry, but it's true."

"That's fair," Sybil admitted.

"What could I say about you?"

Sybil ignored the question for what indeed could her nephew say.

She glanced out the window as they passed by what had been her intended first stop.

Sybil turned to face her nephew.

"What about Cheville? What can you tell me about her?"

"She's here."

"Obviously."

"She can tell you herself."

"I'd rather hear it from you."

"Why?"

"So would I," Cheville contributed.

"We are agreed. How wonderful."

He considered his options.

"Is this how the trip is going to be? Constant questions and girl talk. I signed up to be a driver, see, I even have a hat like a chauffeur."

"You hat is nothing like a chauffeur's headgear, and we are family."

"I heard that recently. I forget where."

Cheville spoke, easing Jason's discomfort.

"Jason and I are in the same situation, Sybil, as you and him. He doesn't really know me."

"But.."

"Yes, there are always buts."

Intense conversations should be carried on obliquely. "Like a tango," thought Cheville, who had never danced a tango.

Sybil nodded silently, understanding that the topic of family was too sensitive for the couple. For her too, she thought, glad to have gotten the awkwardness of this novel situation into the open and thrown from the van.

This could still be her trip. Family or no family aboard.

Caleb watched silently as they passed what could have been the stop, the final stop.

"I wish adults had an off button," he thought fervently.

Sybil was anxious to talk. If not about herself, she would find another topic, one less sensitive.

"I hear so much about remote jobs."

"I'm exhausted from living remote," Cheville responded, wishing that she had said something else, anything less personal and whiny. "I'm being sybilized," she told herself.

"Oh," Sybil said in a surprised voice.

"For you this trip is not really a vacation. If I had known that."

"We appreciate your invitation. It's fun. Forget what I said."

"What were you going to say? I don't want you to regret having asked us to come along."

"I forget now. Anyway, regrets are best left on the side of the road for the trash collector."

Cheville felt guilty and reverted back to Sybil's favorite topics: herself and men.

"Your friend from last night seemed nice."

Sybil laughed.

"You are so polite, maybe I should call you Aunt Cheville."

"He was a bit young," said Jason

"Rather tall too," Cheville hastened to add.

"Men are all a bit and too."

Sybil continued.

"They aren't perfect. Why do you think God came out very soon with version two of humans?"

"It depends."

"Whatever. You have your answer and I have the correct one. Notice however, that there has been no version three, Aunt Cheville."

Cheville blushed and decided to be more direct.

"You pick up men."

"I scoop them up, like this," Sybil said twisting her wrist and closing it into a gentle fist as she swung her arm.

"And I set them back down, none the worse for wear. I may even polish a few of them, the dusty ones."

"What does that mean exactly?"

"Meeting men is stopping by a flea market. I go to those empty attics for amusement. You won't find any bargains on offer. Any jewels are plate. Still, it its pleasurable to pretend, maybe to dream., to reflect on what was once, what once might have been. Its hindsight, bittersweet because it echoes failure, quantifies the passage of time."

"The disappearance of prime?"

"Well put."

"But you replace the object, whatever it was, despite your longing to retain it a while longer, and step away to the next table."

"Or town."

"Or town."

"Your own 100-mile-long yard sale."

"A bit further than that for us."

"For you."

"There is only one headliner per life, dear boy. To each his own, as they say."

"Joy is overrated, contentment is underrated."

"Oh, that's right. You are the generation of just say no. We may have created it, but you had to live it."

"Jason, all of Sybil's advice applies to you, none of it to her."

"What of it? Different times call for new behavior."

"Those are just words."

"Most things are. But you correct."

"Jason, just say no was your mantra. It's just words unless you act on it. Prayers should be self-directed, otherwise they are wasted. In my generation's case, our motto was just say yes."

"And you took it to heart," Cheville added from the rear."

"Yes, yes, yes," she squealed, then put her hands over her mouth and shifted suggestively in the seat.

The motion distracted Caleb from his electrons long enough to utter,

"What's wrong?"

"Nothing, Caleb, just a case of hiccups."

"Caleb is still a kid, Aunt Sybil."

"Yes. I realize that he is just a kid, young, young and young. Healthy, indefatigable, unburdened by responsibility. Caleb is approaching his prime as a human being."

80

"Just like me," Jason exclaimed proudly. "Except that I'm in my prime."

"Hah!" Cheville exclaimed in turn.

"It doesn't endure very long in males. Get over it, Jason, you've gotten over it. Most of it. Irresponsibility departs last, like fading scars from childhood. By the way, are you on drugs?"

"No. Of course not."

"You should start."

There was a gasp from Cheville, but Sybil ignored it.

"Irresponsibility is not a virtue at your age. Its unattractive."

"It's essential if I am going to maintain my how did you phrase it, 'prime as a human being'. You can't have it both ways, Aunt Sybil. I am either in my prime and irresponsible or, he stumbled with his thought, leaving an opportunity for Cheville to furnish, "the opposite, responsible and declining."

"I choose prime," Jason said, nodding at Cheville's words.

"It's not a choice, definitely not yours."

"I disagree. I take responsibility for being irresponsible."

"You are a different person these days," Cheville observed.

"Caleb hasn't been alive long, so he hasn't become someone else. He can only pretend."

"Don't we all."

"I don't."

Cheville and Jason laughed at what they took as a joke.

"When do you stop becoming someone else, Aunt Sybil?" Caleb asked.

Sybil was used to uncomfortable questions emanating from the back of her mind, not being aced to her from the rear of a used Honda.

"This one is for you, Jason," Sybil deflected the serve to him.

"Why me? You're older."

"You have years enough to respond to the boy."

"You know more than I do."

"I do."

"Well?" Sybil persisted.

"Next year, Caleb. A year from now."

Seeing the quizzical look on his companions' faces, he added,

"That's my answer. I'll stop changing in a year."

"Next week would be better," Cheville decided.

He sighed. Sybil recognized the expression; she had seen it innumerable times. It said, 'That's my answer, I hope its adequate.'

"I think never, Caleb."

"That's terrible," Cheville responded immediately.

"Do you truly believe that you never become yourself?"

Sybil said nothing, content to have her answer stand on its own.

"I am happy as I am," Caleb said and returned to his electronic world.

"My turn for music," Jason said, and took the women to his.

It was going to be a quiet evening. Caleb and Jason wanted to watch a sports contest. It is what passes for quality male time.

Sybil suggested a girl's night, an offer Cheville found compelling in its dark attraction.

"I'll be good," she explained to Jason and his girlfriend.

"Good in the sense that I understand good?"

"Good in the sense that most people understand the term. I can't speak to your morals. Your girlfriend will be with me at all times, but Cheville will be on her own."

"What else is new?" Cheville said, directing her question more to Jason than Sybil.

"I really do want a quiet evening."

"Ok, thanks. Caleb and I want the same.

"I make sacrifices, which is simply my nature."

Jason and the boy left them, and the two women strolled towards the bar.

"Young or old, men are a rude product, many examples crude by their own design. But they can be cute."

"You say that like they're kittens."

"It's easier than with kittens. It's not cruel to leave them on the shoulder of a country road."

"Like regrets."

"Like regret. Someone may stop and pick up my regret and be happy ever after with it."

Cheville nodded knowingly.

"I told Jason the truth. I'm exhausted, I need a quiet evening."

"Really?"

"The best time to go to a bad restaurant is when you're not hungry."

They entered and sat at two stools at the far end of the bar.

"I've made an interactive museum of my life. No entry fees, and it is open seven day a week, including holidays. I'm closed tonight."

"I'm not sure my life would rate a showcase let alone a museum. Each morning I find myself further and further from the center of things. I'm nearer and nearer the edge, from where I'll plummet and disappear."

"I've made my own center," Sybil said proudly, "this two-meter radius around me."

"And that is where you find your men, like the one from last night."

"He had a very attractive quality in a man of his age, any age really."

"Endurance?"

"Don't make me laugh."

"Performance?"

"Don't make me cry."

"What's left?" Cheville asked, then guessed, "Staying awake?"

"You're running out of wishes."

"Staying?"

"I don't have all night, Cheville."

"I already said that as one of my guesses," teased Cheville.

"Names."

"His?"

"He remembered my name during and afterwards. Being remembered counts for a great deal."

"Are you two related?" the first man asked. They laughed and he dropped the gambit, hesitant to pursue.

"We are sisters," Sybil said, and the two women laughed, soon joined by the man.

"Really? That was what I thought," he replied, but it was obvious that it was not what he thought.

"It's nice to know where you stand."

"You know where you stand with my sister Sybil, or more accurately you know that she is standing atop you."

He did not understand Cheville's comment, which made for three of them.

The man was paradoxically both interesting and boring. He either believed the fantasies that he related, or he was simply attempting to impress these non-sisters. In either case, he was well within the bell curve's embrace.

"Or crazy," Sybil concluded. "In brief, male normal."

The normal male, Eddy by name was a bit of self-described new ager, part mystic and part hockey fan.

His main claim to self-fame was his ability to hypnotize himself.

"I used to go into a self-induced trancelike state. I did it in childhood numerous times, but had long ago abandoned it, as it was too frightening."

"I used to hide under the covers, which was frightening too," Cheville said, hiding the mockery from her voice.

"Today, I would compare it to a high, not in that it brought euphoria, but because it altered my perception of reality to the point that a new reality was superimposed on what passed for day-to-day normalcy. One moment I was in this world, where things behave as they are supposed to behave, and the next"

"Yes?"

"Different."

"Sybil, I wonder if all three of us are related?"

"Different in what way, Eddy?"

"Sounds were more distinct, they slowed nearly imperceptibly, and the world vibrated, not losing focus, but it neared and withdrew, like a breath. The air was not chilled, but chilling. It was like a foreign world, where its physics distorted the functioning of every sense."

"Sybil, that sounds like your story from last night."

The older woman wanted to kick her younger companion. Did Cheville really want to go watch some sportsball game with the boys? This was not the Oscars, but it was free. He might even buy them a drink.

"How did you do this, Eddy?"

"I don't know. It was easy enough, child's play if you excuse the pun, if the room I occupied was, oh, not dark, but shaded, quiet. I could slip in to with little preparation. I use that word, when its more accurate to say that I simply let myself go."

"Why did you stop, Eddy?" Cheville asked, finally following Sybil's lead.

"I feared that someday I would not be able to return. No one ever mentioned anything similar, so

I thought it odd. I never spoke of it myself. I would be thought odd, crazy."

"And now?"

"I don't care. Maybe because I am odd and or crazy. Or maybe the world is crazy and what concern is one more oddity in it."

"It was travel without physical movement?"

"Yes."

"A change in perspective without a change in position?"

"That describes it pretty well."

"Maybe it was your diet. Or you were just an odd kid."

Sybil added, "I didn't mean it like that. Strange things happen."

"To you?"

"You don't know the half of it Eddy," replied Cheville.

"Nor do you, dear sister," said Sybil, and Cheville shivered.

"I knew a man who said that he'd been murdered."

"What happened to him?"

"He died."

"Hmm," Eddy uttered.

"Later, he died. Not when he had been murdered of course. The doctors brought him back."

"Only to die later?"

"Much later. Unmurdered, I'm sure. But dead just the same. It just goes to show."

"To show what?"

"Something, anything. You decide."

"It's your story, Sybil," Eddy protested.

"No. It was his."

"What does it show you? This double death," persisted Eddy

"I haven't reached a conclusion. Not yet."

"What do you think Cheville?" asked Eddy, searching for help.

"No matter how often you die, you only have one life."

"The last die is final, is what I think," Eddy concluded.

Eddy left a few minutes later, disappointed, but pleased, that he had not heard a story better than the one he had recounted. Maybe tomorrow.

"You can deduce a great deal from a man's car."

"Oh really?"

"Such as what?"

"To begin with, does he own a car? And the list goes on from there.

Is it clean on the inside? Any old damage?"

"Indicating what?"

"Any toys or fast-food remnants in the back seat?"

"That one is obvious."

"Does it smell of tobacco?"

"Or perfume?"

"You are catching on. And then there is the trunk, the obvious hiding place of all things telling."

"So, it pays for a man to rent a car for the first date," Cheville piped in.

"Not really," Sybil replied.

"The car can be a wreck, but still worth a short joy ride."

"You are incorrigible, Sybil."

"I hope so. It's like making Pope and becoming infallible."

She paused, then added.

"Does it work for a woman's minivan?"

"Only a man would wait so long to trust his own judgement in all things. Women are born that way

He sported a grizzled beard, the sort of several days' growth that twentysomethings cultivate, but which comes slovenly naturally to sixty somethings, when indifference is genuine, not feigned.

As to the gap in his lower front teeth she had no philosophical explanation, only the unspoken suggestion that he have it remedied.

The man was loud and his voice constantly on the verge of breaking, his mouth severely lacking in vocabulary

His utterances consisted of a few crackling phrases repeatedly like the dance steps of a debutant dancer, or the hand motions of a sign language imposter at a eulogy.

Another glass of wine might improve the situation either by rendering her briefly dead, or temporarily courageous where she could insult him into leaving.

She caught the bartender's attention long enough to order a nine ounce pour of Blue-Eyed Boy.

The bar was nearly deserted but had been when the second man had arrived. The normal multitude of conversations, in which no single discussion was decipherable, was absent, offering no white noise to mask his.

He did not rise to the level of boor
"I ordered a seven and seven," he said as way of introduction.

"What is that?" Cheville asked politely.

"She knows what it is," the man responded, nodding to the approaching bartender.

"I speak boomer," the bearer of drinks said with a smile to Cheville.

"Was it a crash course?" Sybil asked.

"She is a good student," the man said.

"She is paid to learn."

"A plus," he awarded, a sip latter.

"Anything for you, miss?" offered the man.

Cheville was pleased to have been missed, and replied, "Bitcoin."

"Ok," the bartender said, and moved on down the bar.

"Nothing," she said in answer to his perplexed looks. "We speak millennial."

Sybil regarded him steadily, unemotionally. Her gaze combined attributes of a bird of prey, and the silent passion of an artist.

He was a specimen to be studied as if he was a static display, a species sample already taxidermized.

A young blonde woman in baggy jeans, faded to pastel, and a light pink pullover, equally roomy, arrived and sat at the bar, near enough to the man to say hello, far enough away to say, 'no thanks.' Regardless his attention was drawn to her, despite her lack of embellishments.

"She could use some adornment, some embellishment," Sybil confided to Cheville.

"Such as you have?"

"I told you; this is my day off."

"Her clothes are modest. What of it?"

"Even the Chinese trashed those suits from the 50s and 60s for Dior. Mao is so passe. Look at the Pope, versus monks. They attend the same club, but they don't share a tailor."

The blonde finished her drink and left, followed a few minutes later by the man whose name they had not learned.

"Sybil, do you find it weird?"

Her companion regarded her with curiosity.

"All of this...auditioning."

"I know," Sybil replied flatly.

"I thought it was only me."

"It is only you."

It was Cheville's turn to be perplexed.

"I know the term. I understand the word auditioning. What I find odd is that you find this weird. We have more in common than you admit. Slut life for the two of us."

Sybil raised her glass. Cheville frowned but she said nothing

"Men are the same. Don't you agree?

Men are always the same. You must have learned that by now, Cheville. Everywhere the same.

On the other hand, I can be someone different. Isn't that pure American? It's easier to pretend for one rather than reimagine for an entire gender."

The third man was quiet. He said hello and nothing more. He wrote a few words in a small notebook which he then placed it in the inside pocket of his jacket.

He sat back, quiet, contented.

Sybil had seen his type before and was not going to let him get away with ignoring her. She ran through her collection of lines and rejected them all.

He was not her type, she knew it instinctively, and besides she was off duty.

"Hi, I'm Sybil, and this is Cheville."

He did not ask them to define their relationship, nor he compliment or endeavor to entice them via insult.

He was unique but implausible. He looked and reminded her of no other man, least of all himself

"It's easier to talk to strangers. They are too polite or ignorant of our faults to call BS. They have enough of their own. What do you think?" she left his name unspoken, hoping that he would fill in the blank.

"William," he obliged.

"What do you do, William?", Sybil asked, wishing that she was Cheville so that she could kick Sybil.

"I'm retired and I write."

"Me too, that is I'm retired."

"Did you fear it?"

Sybil considered the question.

"It's an excellent motivator, you know," he said.

"Retirement? It hasn't motivated me in the least."

"Fear. It is one of the two great motivators."

"Oh, fear. Yes, it must be."

"For men," Sybil did not add.

"Fear and"

"Sex."

"That makes three. I was going to say greed."

He considered Sybil's answer and continued.

"You aren't the retiring type yourself. Sex," he repeated and laughed pleasantly."

"Sex is not a laughing matter. Not usually. Not at first."

"Not with you, I imagine."

"Imagining is doing."

Observing that she had his interest, Sybil changed the subject. They were both retired. They had time. Even if this was only a practice round.

"You mentioned fear."

"Did I? That seems like long ago."

"Were you concerned that retirement would change you? Did you imagine that once you were no longer what you once were, you would have to settle for something different, perhaps something less?"

"Sometimes imagining is not doing," he replied, smiling.

"We have time," he added, echoing her thoughts.

"To answer your question, Sybil, it was the exact opposite. I was afraid that retirement would not change me. I would remain unaltered, a milk wagon horse in an open field, bereft of familiar urban stops and unable to smell the flowers, let alone free to munch them.

I no longer wanted to be what I once was, as you so succinctly put it. Whatever that was. I was proud of it, content. If there was to be no change, no clear demarcation to the novel, then why retire? I would be stuck in a senior version of sophomore year high school, Groundhog Day without end."

"Most people enjoy that film," Cheville interjected, then sat back, wishing that she had remained a spectator in this drama.

"It's a movie. It ended"

"Did you like it?" Sybil asked.

It really was quite amazing, unique. Darn."

"What?"

"I used the A word."

"Which? Amazing?"

"Yes. That word and racist are so overused." He sighed.

"Everything is amazing or racist."

"Combine them."

"What?" William asked, perplexed.

"The A word and what I guess you call the R word."

The man nodded at the mention of the letter.

"So, combine the two and just make up new words. If you want to say something is 'amazing', sorry but stay with me, you could say rarazing, or araciming. New words must begin somewhere."

"You're right. It's a wonderful idea. This is.." he reflected for a moment.

"Ramaist."

William perked up. He had just returned from an art tour in France.

"Have you been there before?"

"Oh sure, I've to Europe a dozen times, but I've missed sights a few hours away."

"I've seen neither."

"You have time," he said, three magical words with so much promise.

"Are you working on a book?" Cheville asked, refusing to be invisible.

"Yes, I should leave you ladies and attend to it now." He made a motion to leave.

"I'm traveling with my nephew," Sybil said, concerned that he might leave.

"He'd like to be a writer."

"Well," William said, "you have the prettiest nephew I've ever seen."

Sybil laughed.

"He is a nondrinker, a nonsmoker, and a nonworker. If he could survive that way, he would be a non-eater as well."

Cheville leaned back, grateful for the stool's back support.

"He is also a non-learner, beyond the bare minimum. He can read and write. He absorbs somethings apparently, but as far as I can detect, he does nothing."

"Perfect, he is a blank slate. Let's have another drink. We have time and you can tell me about your nephew. Now he sounds ramaist."

"Maybe he is a thinker," Sybil said as their laughter subsided.

"You may be on to something."

"Rodin's sculpture was nothing more than a rock, and a century or so later it still is."

"Nephew is keeping pace."

"It's art, but really it remains a rock."

"Er, yes."

"It thinks regardless of its form."

"You have a point," Sybil agreed, but not sure what it was.

"But even a rock takes a tumble once in a while," Sybil flirted.

"Raramazing."

William stood.

"Again ladies, it was a pleasure, but I need to go upstairs and work a bit. Few things can deter a writer from finishing a scene."

"Discarded lingerie?"

He considered the offer posed as a question.

"Only if it furthers the scene. I don't see that it does."

He looked steadily at Sybil.

"No," he said a moment later, "it doesn't."

With a courteous, "Good night, ladies," he left them.

Sybil was speechless and motionless, as if she had been punched senseless and had not yet tumbled to the floor.

She was not used to such rejection, but she had limited experience with dedicated writers, for they are among the most brutal of humans. They lack the emotion about which they scribble so diligently.

"I'm going to bed," she said to Cheville.
"Alone."

CHAPTER ELEVEN

There was a light mist, and Jason had been driving extra cautiously.

"This slow life is not bad," he said.

"No traffic, no businesses, just us and the scenery."

"I don't understand why we stopped at a cemetery in Whitland. I enjoyed the game with Caleb, but you must admit it was odd."

"Life is odd. Cemeteries are one of the few remaining places where a person can be safely stupid. You might be at home everywhere, most people aren't.

I discovered mine."

Jason and Cheville exchanged a glance in the mirror,

"But those sorts of locations have been internetted to extinction like a species of tropical butterfly, magical in its beauty and consequently pursued to nonexistence."

Sybil paused for breath.

"Let's get death off the table. It is in the past. No looking in the rear-view mirror. Except you Jason."

"Sure. This is the life, isn't it Caleb", but the boy's ears were filled with buds.

Sybil nevertheless returned to talk of graves.

"The best cemetery in the world. What a bizarre category when you think about it. It's a place to avoid, despite the number of blue ribbons it may boast."

"Got it," Jason said. "There are sights to see and people to avoid."

"Unless they are horizontal?" Cheville asked

Jason blushed at the double-entendre.

"Don't be a child, dear nephew. Politeness and modesty don't become men or you."

"I meant horizontal as in dead."

The continued conversation had attracted Caleb's attention and he removed his hearing disablers.

"Now they are polite, the dead that is. They let me have the last word."

"They leave you all the words."

"Why visit them?" Cheville asked.

"I'm not sure," she answered

"But it's a good, serious question. Give me a moment."

She turned and stared out the passenger window as the scenery passed slowly by.

Cheville thought that Sybil had either elected to ignore the question, or fallen asleep, when she stirred and turned back to face Cheville.

"Why visit them? I'm not sure. Maybe to see if anyone is at home."

"Where would they go?" the boy asked, his question as serious as that rear seat companion.

"Where indeed? Are they traveling like us?"

The boy frowned in puzzlement. Adults bounced between mystery and baby babble.

Did they talk like this among themselves? If so, he would definitely pass on adulthood.

"Or are they here? I wait to see if one will break their vow of silence. A complaint or a whiff of bravado would be welcome."

Jason and Cheville smiled at this remark.

"Not a ....boo," she exclaimed, causing her three companions to jump in unison.

"Nothing. You would think that every cemetery would rent to at least one ghost."

"But?"

"Nothing. Gettysburg and Normandy, nothing. I asked what's his name, you know he went to France every year. He never saw squat as far as phantoms."

The conversation ended, they each retreated into the separate thoughts.

"Pull in up there," Sybil said, a grimace on her face.

"Where, at the cemetery?"

"Yes."

"You have got to be kidding, Aunt Sybil. You might need help, but you are not going to get it here. What is it with you and graveyards? "

"More good luck?" asked Cheville.

"Potty break this time," she replied in an attempt at humor.

"Seriously?"

"Seriously. I need to go to the bathroom."

"They won't have one."

"I'll make do."

The cemetery was absent of living souls at that hour, except for two men occupied with an excavation.

"Stop here and let me out. I'll go ask them."

"Ask them what?" Jason nearly shouted.

"Never you mind. It looks like they are nearly done, given the size of that mound of dirt. They start early for a stranger who is late."

With that, she exited the vehicle and walked, in a manner that was both slow and hurried, to the open grave, her handbag in her left hand.

The three occupants of the Odyssey watched silently as Sybil and the two men held a brief conversation. They could not hear the words but noticed a few hand motions by Sybil to the open tomb, and a nod and a shrug on the part of the two men. Sybil handed her purse to one of the men.

Sybil swiveled slowly to face the opened grave, and suddenly disappeared from sight, followed quickly by the reappearance of her right hand with an upright thumb.

The hand reopened, and the shorter of the two men placed the strap of Sybil's purse into it.

The pair of gravediggers turned their backs and moved a few paces away. One of them lit a cigarette.

After what seemed like an eternity, the men turned around again and approached the grave.

The taller one reached down to retrieve the purse that extended from below the surface of the opening. After a moment's hesitation, he slung it over his shoulder. The men then each extended an arm downward and lifted Sybil effortlessly from the rectangular hole.

The van's trio exhaled collectively.

"She's so cool," Caleb exclaimed.

Sybil gave each of the men a peck on the cheek and returned to vehicle at a graceful walk.

As Jason drove them slowly back to the paved road, Cheville asked,

"You didn't?"

"The gravediggers didn't care one way or the other. They are last responders, don't you know? They wouldn't turn their back on a woman in need."

"That is exactly what they did," Cheville said, attempting to suppress a laugh.

"So you..", she began.

"Theirs is a thankless and complaint free career, with no repeat customers. I think I made their day."

"So, you?"

"I did indeed. I christened it."

CHAPTER TWELVE

Maurice kissed Sybil on both cheeks, stepped into his 80s Buick convertible, and drove away slowly.

"Our next stop is Lumbia?" Jason asked in response to his aunt's direction.

He turned to face Sybil.

"Where the f___ is that?"

"The slap was immediate and thunderous inside the confines of the van."

"What the f___?"

Another slap followed to the same cheek

"You'll thank me later," Sybil said calmly, as she turned to the front and reached across her body with her left arm to find the seat belt.

"It's not far," she added.

"Is that your version of an apology?"

"A few hours at most."

"I think that you are going to enjoy the next few days. We have a surprise planned."

"We do? Oh good. The fun was bound to start soon."

"I'm as sorry for the slaps as you are for your language," Sybil said, offering the best she could in way of apology, but more concerned that she might lose her driver.

"Is Lumbia known for its men?" Cheville teased. Maybe there is more than one available."

"One is enough," Sybil answered.

"And you aren't too old to smack either Cheville."

"That isn't what I meant."

Caleb spoke up.

"It's like an Amish community. With a restaurant and some kind of playhouse. That must be for girls."

"It sounds wonderful," Jason said sarcastically. Maybe I'll push old Silver here to forty-six miles per hour to get there sooner,

"I think that we all need some downtime."

"Downtime from what?" Jason asked, incredulous.

"I know I do."

They pulled into Lumbia, or more accurately, they stopped at the crossroads where the hotel was situated.

The hotel was nothing special, except for the Grand Suite that Sybil had rented.

"Where is our room?" Jason asked.

"Whatever it is, we can switch."

"There is no other room. This is a suite. It's for all of us."

The silence reflected their excitement.

"I won't show you my part of the suite, I know it would only disappoint you."

Jason looked around the suite. It was gorgeous, with Sybil's portion obscured by a wall that reached nearly to the ceiling and extended almost to the window.

"A screen, not a wall," he said aloud to himself.

"It reminds me of a stage, or a film set."

106

Caleb scurried to the bathroom, having learned that it was best to preempt the two women.

The suite did resemble the set of a play, with a half wall separating the bedroom from the living room and small kitchen. Two doors led to the shared bathroom, designed to generate awkward situations.

"This is fine, Sybil, thank you. It's very peaceful being on the top floor."

"I'll have sufficient privacy, as will you."

"The kid is a ball and chain, nothing will happen."

"He's here Jason, so something has already happened."

Later as they prepared for sleep, Jason set up the sofa bed and fold out cot.

"This one could have come from FEMA or a former prison. Its good enough for Caleb."

"No, the prison bed is for you, 'dear nephew'", Cheville advised.

"What the?"

Jason closed his mouth in seeing Cheville's upraised hand.

"No hanky panky tonight, not for nephew and not for aunty."

CHAPTER THIRTEEN

After a day viewing more arcane sights, Jason prepared to continue the journey westward. He was surprised when Sybil told him to turn left.

"East?"

"Yes. We are returning to Lumbia."

"You liked it that much.?"

"It was nice."

"Why go back? Nice is nice, but." he left the question unfinished.

"Dry cleaning."

"We can drop it off anywhere."

"I already did. Yesterday. In Lumbia."

"Then why did we check out, if you knew we were returning?"

"Its fine, Jason," Cheville interjected, ending the interrogation.

"It was nice. Are we sharing the same suite as last night?"

"Yes," answered Sybil.

"I wasn't sure at first, but as things turned out...".

"I made the reservation," Caleb said proudly.

"Yes, he did. I like having a private travel agent," Sybil said.

"So, to be clear, we are staying in Lumbia just like last night? Like Groundhog Day."

"Yes. I wanted to have dry cleaning and laundry done."

The existence of dry cleaners had been a revelation to Caleb. Sybil was pleased to have introduced something new and now of such importance to the boy, the younger boy.

"We need to swing by and retrieve my fresh laundry. We may as well stay overnight."

"Fresh laundry," Jason repeated. He nearly used a different adjective beginning with the letter F, but he recalled the sting of her slap. How many days ago was that? He was beginning to lose count. It was pleasant

Still. It was silly, no demeaning for Sybil to censor his vocabulary. His language was no worse than his friends.

He blushed deep crimson, as if he'd in fact been slapped.

"Are you OK, Jason?" Sybil asked.

"I'm getting there."

"You're doing what?"

"I'm doing nothing," he pouted

"We are returning to town. Call it a detour."

"But why? All this fuss over some laundry?"

"We're confined in this van. Hygiene and clean clothes are essential."

"Confined? The Odyssey barely reaches operating temperature before we call it a day."

"Then this side trip won't delay us."

"This trip is nothing but a series of delays."

"Isn't it wonderful?"

Jason refused to admit that he agreed, so he said nothing.

It was pleasant, but he felt that he was circling an airport, and even though he had never flown, he could imagine the feeling of impatience, knowing that he had important business on the ground below, whatever business that might happen to be.

He didn't see the logic of this voyage to nowhere, he wanted to protest, but he found himself enjoying the lack of purpose. It fit his nature, but he had begun to feel tinges of guilt. Maybe his nature needed corrections, and small daily tweaks that mirrored their daily jaunts were helpful.

Cheville echoed his unspoken words.

"This is different than any other road trip I've seen or read. It's more like.."

"Like what?"

"A rehearsal?" She said hesitantly

"Is that bad?" Cheville added.

"A road trip rehearsal? It seems positively un-American. To be honest, the old America doesn't exist any longer. Where have you two been living for the past ten years?"

"In Pittsburgh," Jason replied

"Pittsburgh? Cities are doped up and unable to function. They pretend to pass laws and we pretend to obey them."

"It's not that bad."

"Even a chronic bitcher such as myself has valid complaints now and again. The last time I saw someone reading a book in public, I took him for a thumper or a time traveler from the past.

And you?" Sybil directed the question to Cheville.

"A town just like Brentville."

"You've been lucky then, young lady. This is our road trip, unique and maybe the first of its kind.

Short days and clean clothes. Maybe it's the new American way."

CHAPTER FOURTEEN

Jason and Cheville woke early the next morning, and without showering, or even brushing their teeth, they agreed to take the elevator down to the lobby for coffee and conversation, while the chaperones were still sleeping.

"The bookends won't be awake for another hour," Cheville said, as they slipped away, using their private nickname for their two absent companions.

"Sybil needs downtime from having had too much downtime."

"And we are stuck here in a small town on this small planet."

"How is it different from the past few days, or past few years if you think about it. And I do think about it."

Jason knew Cheville well enough to know when to let her rant.

"Jason, whatever we have," she began and then stopped.

"I would say that whatever we have isn't working out as planned. But that would be a lie, as there is not and there never has been a plan. I don't know maybe Caleb has a plan."

"I have no doubt that he has a plan," Jason said with his most endearing smile.

"It is the plan of a child, and given the past few days, I suspect that it includes Sybil and not us."

She went on,

"She's new, she's funny in the annoying way that children find irresistible. It works on you, too. She has money, she can provide all the toys that boys find attractive."

Jason remained silent, knowing that there was more to come.

"As for me, I've done my bit. More than I ever expected."

She looked around the lobby, giving him time to absorb her words. She did not see it when he nodded his head in agreement.

"And I'll continue to do it for a while longer. No, don't ask me what constitutes a while, I can't give you a commitment. You understand."

This time she observed his head movement.

"More than an hour, less than a month. But I am not inviting you to a conversation that we should have had long ago. I was unsure about this trip. It's another delay, play time when there is genuine work to be completed."

"We can stop the trip today. An hour from now. We can be back in Brentville in three days if we take the Conestoga trail, tonight if we follow freeways like normal people."

"Your aunt has been bossy, annoying. I could continue listing her character flaws, but you know her better than I. It would be an additional waste of time.

"If,".

"But she has taught me to act selfishly, and for that alone the trip has been invaluable."

"Then wait until this trip is concluded."

"I won't guarantee that I'll stay for the duration."

"You may learn something else about yourself."

"Sybil collecting men as some folks collect postcards. See told me that men offer themselves at a discount, their testosterone undermines their negotiating skills, were her exact words. As if she is some sexual guru on television."

"We will leave her."

Cheville looked at him expectantly.

"I will leave her a note, one beautifully written. She is bound to forgive our desertion if we use correct punctuation. I can use the hotel computer to spell check it and then copy it by hand. I can't text her, that is certain. We'll be back in two days."

"What is the point of leaving if we intend to return in two days?"

"I will tell her two days, but who knows. I don't. It gives us time."

"Time for what? We have time now. Where would we go?"

"You are sounding like Sybil!"

"Me sounding like Sybil? You are her nephew, and it is beginning to show. You push me in a direction without any input, and advance until you decide to stop. It is all so unplanned. It's just random and hap hazardous motion with no destination in mind. At least with Sybil she is willing and able to pay for it.

How far can we go? A few hundred miles? We don't have enough gas money to return to Brentville. We're stuck. You must realize that."

Jason shrugged.

"You have no goal. Like your life up to now."

He looked sharply at Cheville.

Cheville spoke again, softly.

"Like my life up to now. The same for the both of us. What do you want?"

"What do you want?"

"What do I want? I don't know. Not this."

"It's not bad."

"Like you said, its motion without a destination."

"Let's think more about this. We have time."

"I told you Jason, that this is not a negotiation, but a notification. I won't promise you anything."

Jason said nothing.

"I can do either what I want, or what you want. That's not a difficult choice.

Please understand that you are not registered to vote in my life."

"And Caleb?"

"Hi," Caleb said, appearing at Jason's side.

"You and Cheville look like you just woke up."

CHAPTER FIFTEEN

"Where is the next town, Aunt Sybil?", Caleb asked.

"The next town? Aunt Sybil has restricted us to second rate villages. I'm beginning to miss red lights. I may freeze at the next one we come across. I'm feeling old and out of date. Expired, you might say."

Jason's words were in jest, and spurred Sybil to retort,

"It's me who is rapidly aging out of America. I was best before Y2K. Maybe I can have that tattooed on my ass in the next town."

"You may need to settle for a blacksmith and a hot butt brand."

"Seriously though, where to?"

"We are going to a family reunion."

"Whose?" Cheville asked logically.

"We aren't even a family ourselves," Jason remarked.

"Then it is time to see what one is."

"Whose?" Cheville repeated like a lispsy owl.

"The Deiters."

"I thought that you hated reunions. Mom told me that."

"I have distant relatives, who up until recently I've done my best to keep distant. These are strangers, so I've made an exception."

"Who are they?"

"Why them?"

"We can play twenty questions, or I can tell you the plan and let you ask questions afterward."

"I prefer twenty questions," Jason said just to be obstinate.

"We have plenty of time, so I agree with Jason. It might even be fun."

"The reunion?"

"Asking questions about this insane idea. The reunion will be agony."

"Why do we have to go?"

"Don't waste any of your twenty questions on foolish ones. Sybil has commanded," Cheville said, her voice neutral.

"You're wrong, Cheville."

"About what?"

"We don't have much time. We will be there in fifteen minutes."

"This is beyond insane."

"Once you pass insanity, you arrive at delirious happiness. Also known as a lead role on Broadway."

"I can't believe this."

"Then don't. Just read the notes."

She passed pages to Cheville, then directed Jason to pull over, before handing him his.

"What are these?"

"Background on who you are, or more accurately, who you will be for the next few hours."

"A script?"

"It's not that detailed, this is more ad hoc."

Jason could not prevent himself from perusing the notes.

"Jason Deiter, 27, married to Cheville, one child, Caleb. Runs a bed and breakfast and a small lumber mill in, what is this town? I've never heard of it."

"No one has."

"Word of mouth, no internet presence. At least we aren't Amish."

"Be glad that you don't already have a beard."

"By the way, here are your wedding rings."

"This is too much," Cheville exclaimed.

"Don't worry, you can thank me later."

"Whose," she began, but Sybil answered.

"It was Caleb's idea."

"I doubt that."

"Why do you think I made an exception. Really it was, he selected the Deiter family. They are having quite a spread of food, and it's a huge family."

"But it was your idea to crash a stranger's reunion. Caleb's research was at your instigation."

"Look, let's not waste time on reviews before the curtain even rises. Take these," she added, handing each of them an empty plastic grocery bag.

"If it goes poorly, grab some food before we are ejected. I am getting tired of roadside cuisine. I swear that some of it must be roadkill."

"Crashing a stranger's reunion."

"Don't be so conventional, mister crypto. Who knows, this might be a preunion."

"What does that mean?"

"Caleb might meet his future wife there."

"Ugh," Caleb responded.

"So, we aren't crashing a reunion, we are simply arriving early. Above all, don't forget to take a doggie bag."

"Woof, woof," answered Cheville with a laugh.

CHAPTER SIXTEEN

For once, Jason was happy to be driving a minivan. Without direction from Sybil, he pulled into the open field that served as parking for the Deiter reunion. The temporary lot was well represented with similar vehicles.

Sybil asked to have the hatch released and retrieved from it a rectangular box.

"We can't show up to our reunion empty handed. Here Caleb, take this," the older woman instructed.

"Our reunion?"

"We are family, more or less, and this is a reunion. There are always new family members. Family is like Rome; it wasn't destroyed in one day."

"Or built?"

"Yes, that too. Come on now, we mustn't be late."

And with that, she marched off toward the party.

"What are the donuts for?" Jason asked, indicating the box that Caleb was carrying so carefully.

"We can't arrive empty handed," Sybil admonished.

"That would be tacky."

"Where did you get the donuts?" Cheville inquired.

"From that shop across from the hotel we stayed at last night. They were closing for the evening and the donuts were half price."

"Stale donuts?" asked Jason.

"Bring a cheap gift when you crash a party," Cheville said to Caleb.

"Pay attention to your Aunt Sybil's lessons and you will do just fine in life," she added.

"I'm sure that the Deiters would be pleased to know that their reunion is attractive enough to crash."

"Should we tell them beforehand?" Jason teased.

"It can wait."

"It's the thought that counts," Sybil added in reply to Cheville's jab.

"People remember the thought, not the gift."

"That is so not true," Cheville exclaimed, laughing at the boldness of the untruth.

"The thought that counts," Cheville repeated.

"That idea is as stale and full of holes as your donuts."

The foursome was nearing the reception table, beyond which lay the festivities.

The reunion was in full swing, which meant in this case, that reams of Deiters formed several lines at the well-organized buffet line that stretched from one end to the other of a large canopy.

"There must be over a hundred people here," Cheville said nervously.

"At least," Sybil agreed.

"I am so pleased with the turnout."

"If you are pleased Aunt Sybil, so are we," Jason said sarcastically.

"I'm still your nephew here, aren't I?"

Sybil did not deign to answer the question.

The reception table was staffed by an underling, as anyone of adult age was standing in the chow line. The young Deiter seated before the crashers was more concerned at missing his opportunity under the kitchen canopy, than he was at verifying these late arrivals.

Sybil stopped in front on the boy.

"See," she said, talking to the others over her shoulder, "we're late."

"Better late than never," Cheville replied, suddenly lost in her role.

"Hello young man," Sybil said in her best ex-teacher voice to the gatekeeper.

"You must be one of Rose's boys."

"The boy looked confused," Sybil thought. "Good. He's afraid that I'm going to give him an old woman kiss." She considered doing so but changed her mind.

"Am I right?" she asked the boy.

"My mother is Meghan."

"Of course, I always confuse the two."

Sybil looked at the boy for a few more seconds, still considering bestowing a smooch.

"They've begun eating," Jason prompted his aunt.

"And here you are manning the gate," Sybil said, adding "Brian."

"We've brought some delicious donuts, Brian. Would you like one?" Sybil asked, nudging Caleb to come front and center.

"Caleb, this is your cousin Brian."

"Take two, Brian. I'll ask Meghan to bring you a plate, or at least send someone to relieve you. You're doing important work here. We can fill in these," Sybil said, picking up four nametags.

"You have your hands full."

And with that observation, the four crossed the threshold into the Deiter festivities.

"Just like walking across the southern border," Sybil said.

Sybil quickly disposed of their cover fee on a nearby half empty table.

"Rejects or reserves?" Cheville teased the older woman.

Sybil counseled the other three newly minted Deiters to split up, with each standing in a separate line.

"One of us is certain to succeed," she said with a mischievous grin.

All four completed their line. The meal was as advertised. There were copious amounts of fried and baked chicken, pulled pork, salads and casseroles of all sorts, along with cheeses and desserts, all fresh Cheville commented to Sybil when they happened to cross paths. There were sliced vegetables and juicy watermelon. Coolers overflowed with beverages, soft and alcoholic alike.

They had agreed to not sit together, and, as it turned out, only Sybil faced any questioning. At that was purely due to her age, where she was expected to know something of Deiter history. She had anticipated that hers would be the principal role and that she would be required to carry the troupe. Fortunately she'd had more time to review Caleb's research. The Deiter family was wonderful. She had mentioned to Jason as they sat watching the three-legged race,

"I could join this family, Jason. They are so nice."

"And trusting," her nephew retorted.

"And good cooks."

They were trusting. When pressed by a Deiter on certain topics, she would fall back on her faulty memory, or the standard excuse, 'It was so long ago.'

"The people I remember from my youth, when I attended reunions, are all gone."

That much was true.

Sybil would then sigh and stare into the distance, her regard a mixture of sadness and loneliness.

It worked on Deiters as well as it did the last time that she had been stopped for speeding by a Pennsylvania state trooper.

"Everyone has a grandmother," she told herself, smiling at the memory of the officer's polite warning.

Caleb played with the other children of his age, while Jason and Cheville attached themselves to opposing volleyball teams, venues where conversation was minimal. When the highlight of the familial competition, a scarecrow building contest, was over, Sybil decided that the moment to depart had come.

The multitude of Deiters would soon begin to dwindle, increasing the probability of exposure.

Each gathered a final doggie bag from the buffet and placed the food in the large beach bag that Sybil carried.

"I can carry your bag," Jason offered.

"Thanks, but I'll shoulder it myself, Jason. It's the least that I can do."

A few moments later, as the interlopers rolled away Cheville was hesitant to quit her role, and the extended, if false family, to which it had provided access. She then began to laugh.

"What's funny?" Caleb demanded.

"Months, and years from now when they look at the group photos that were taken, we will remain distant relatives, forever unknown. What will they think?"

The others joined Cheville in laughter, as it was a joke that required no punch line.

CHAPTER SEVENTEEN

It was time for Caleb's music time. The adults had thought nothing of including the boy in the musical rotation but had soon come to dread unanimously that sixty minutes.

He had once asked for channel 174, which happened to be in French.

"No wonder that Caleb thinks Ohio is a foreign country," Jason had joked.

His taste was eclectic, ranging from hip hop to classic, from gospel to preaching.

Sybil's unspoken thought that he chose XM numbers at random was effectively his method. Caleb would pick the route number, or its inverse, distance markers, the time of day.

His current selection was channel sixty-nine, which turned out to be instrumental songs only, the first what Sybil would have termed Hawaiian country.

She recalled one of his less fortuitous choices, having called out a number that resulted in a few seconds of expletive laden modern comedy before Sybil pressed another button, this one also at random.

It was not the periodic transitions from soothing music to redneck or thug preaching that annoyed the adults as much as the fact that more often than not, Caleb sat there wearing his earbuds, exempt from the symphonic scolding.

"We have eaten the last of the reunion food."

"Can Caleb find us another friendly family gathering."

"Not at this hour. We need to stop anyway for gas."

"Yes, we are nearly below three-quarters. This regular gas doesn't get very good mileage," he teased.

"Let's not get gas here."

"Why not?"

Sybil indicated the nearby tanker truck.

"They are filling the underground storage tanks."

"Good, that means fresher fuel."

"It stirs up all the crud and who knows what else."

"I'm sure you don't."

"That can cause all sorts of damage."

"I've never heard anyone complain."

"Aren't there filters along the way?" asked Cheville.

"I fill a can for mowing lawns directly from pumps. I haven't seen any crud."

"You need to get a real job, by the way. Let Caleb mow lawns."

"Caleb?"

"Your boy in the back seat."

"Well,' he began.

"Caleb can't do anything remotely resembling adult behavior."

"He's a child."

"And my mower runs fine."

"Lawnmowers are forgiving."

"So am I."

"You must have gotten lucky."

"Luck follows me like the bag follows the mower. Yep, that's me."

"Cheville, let's go inside for a minute. Would that be alright with you?"

Cheville said nothing but opened the passenger door and stepped out and accompanied Sybil into the store.

"I thought that children like him would be more self-sufficient. Instead he's less."

"Children like him?"

She ignored the anger in Cheville's voice

"Kids in unusual family situations. I suppose that unusual has become the usual."

"He's going to be fine. He's a child," Cheville repeated as way of explanation.

He's going to turn out like my nephew Jason if you don't act soon. Unless you believe that Jason has turned out fine. I suppose that you must."

"Must I?"

The response startled the older woman.

"Jason's whole life has been one unusual family situation after another."

"Has it? He told me once that he and his father didn't see eye to eye."

"They rarely do. It doesn't matter as they become their father regardless.

Men wear their testosterone like steel toed boots. They kick whatever they like and walk unscathed through fire."

Cheville listened.

"We develop calluses."

"You seem to have done well enough with your tankful of estrogen."

"Calluses can be as effective as Red Wings. For when the estrogen just isn't enough."

While Jason filled the tank and checked various fluids and pressures, Sybil and Cheville asked the inside attendant for suggestions.

"Are there any good, local restaurants?"

"We have one. It's called No Substitutions."

"Is it any good?" Sybil asked, emphasizing the last word

"What do they serve?"

"It changes from day to day, but folks seem to like it."

"Are there any others?" Cheville asked helpfully.

"Restaurants? Nope. Only the one."

"Have you been there?"

"Sure."

"Sybil, since there is no alternative."

"Yes, of course, We will eat there."

Jason restarted the engine.

"See? It sounds fine. Like I said, lucky."

"Ok, lucky we found a restaurant," Cheville said.

"I do think that you may have a point, Aunt Sybil. I'll pay closer attention."

"There isn't much else for you to pay for," Cheville quipped.

"I'd hate to be broken down 5 miles from the next hick town."

"I remember the early days of Covid. Gas was so inexpensive. I recall buying it at $1.23 per gallon. That was wonderful."

"I remember it being not wonderful."

"But there was nowhere to go."

There was no response necessary.

"Gas has more than doubled in price."

"And you're taking us on a trip to nowhere."

"You volunteered."

"From one nowhere to another. Repeatedly."

"Just like a Caribbean cruise."

"I haven't taken a cruise, and if this is what they are like, I'll pass."

"What do you suggest, a bigger buffet at Bob Evans?"

"They dropped it."

"You will ridicule whatever I, or Cheville, or Caleb suggest."

"I treat all bad ideas equally. I'm nothing if not fair."

"I haven't offered one idea, and you've already jettisoned it to the shoulder.

"Don't be so sensitive. Jason, tell me. It will pass the time until our upcoming nowhere."

"A city."

"A city?"

"Yes, a city. Not a village, not a hamlet with delusions of townhood. A city. Maybe one with a buffet. Chicago, New York, Los Angeles, Miami."

"You've exhausted the list."

"There are others. Houston. I forgot Houston."

"It's worthy of being forgotten."

"You've visited Houston?"

"Mistake," was Sybil's terse response.

"You visited Houston by mistake?"

"By plane. My going there was the mistake."

"A man?"

"Yes."

"A man who wasn't what you expected?"

"He was exactly what I expected. I'd hoped to be wrong. A mistake."

The restaurant was uncrowded at that time of day, and the hostess' stand was empty, the role assumed by a simple sign reading. 'Please seat yourself.'

Despite the warmth and brightness of the day, or perhaps in response to it, Sybil gravitated to a table for four next to one of the large windows that made up one side of the restaurant.

When the waitress approached to take their beverage order, Sybil requested coffee, decaf.

The waitress, Anna, replied,

"We don't have decaf."

"It's early," Sybil smiled, "regular will be fine."

Jason and Caleb each ordered a Coke, while Cheville chose Diet, no ice.

Sybil perused the menu that his table companions had curtly reviewed. Jason stared off into nothingness, and Cheville watched Caleb, who was inspecting each and every packet of sugar and sweet and low on the table.

"They haven't been tampered with honey," Cheville said.

"It doesn't hurt to check," the boy replied without looking up from his investigatory activity.

"What are you doing Caleb?"

"Checking the packets for," he said quietly, his voice trailing off as he failed to find the right word.

"Caleb, it doesn't matter. You don't use sweetener. If you were the target, they'd have to find another method of poisoning you."

"Like in your Coke," Jason teased, his mind rejoining his body.

Sybil ignored the talk. She'd had plenty of experience with boys of Caleb's age.

She was tempted to tell her nephew not to encourage the boy's behavior, but that could wait for another day.

The menu was limited but sufficient. At the top of the few pages was printed the name of the eatery in large font, No Substitutions, and the same appeared the bottom, in smaller type face.

Anna returned with the drink, placing them accurately on the table.

"Is this Diet?" asked Cheville.

"Yes ma'am."

"I asked for no ice."

Anna either ignored or did not hear Cheville's comment.

"Are you ready to order now?" the server asked politely.

"This has ice in it," Cheville said, indicating her drink with a vertical open hand as a sort of private sign language.

"Yes ma'am," Anna agreed

"A little ice won't hurt you. Caleb is satisfied with his not being compromised. Me too."

Cheville bit her tongue and began scooping handfuls of the slippery ice into their glasses, forcing them to hurriedly drink to keep up with the unexpected avalanche.

Anna stood by patiently, glad that she was paid by the hour. This group was not going to be remembered for their tipping ability.

Cheville picked the last of the offending ice from her Diet and dropped them dramatically into the creamer.

"I don't want anyone to feel left out," she said, and leaned back in her chair, sipping from her drink like an innocent seven-year-old girl.

Sensing that the first monologue of act one, scene one had concluded, the waitress took her cue, and asked Sybil,

"What would you like, ma'am?"

"I'd like a cup of the soup du jour and the chicken sandwich, no bun. And fresh fruit instead of the potato salad.

Sybil noticed that Anna wrote nothing down. It was irritating, as this guaranteed a mix-up. Jason and Cheville each ordered a Caesar salad, with her nephew requesting no croutons and dressing on the side.

"Just like an old married couple," remarked Sybil.

"The same dish," she added.

Jason winked at Cheville but remained silent.

"I want the cheeseburger. And I want an order of fruit."

"You want fruit and fries?" Jason asked the boy.

Caleb nodded vigorously.

"And pie, a slice of apple pie."

"Please," he added.

"Caleb," Jason began, but Sybil cut him off.

"That's fine. He said please."

The meals when they were delivered matched the menu exactly, but those of the adults differed from what they had ordered. Only Caleb's was correct on both counts.

"This is not what I ordered miss, Anna," Sybil objected.

"Neither is mine," Cheville contributed.

Jason voted with the women with a shake of his head. He was content to let them resolve the situation.

For his part, Caleb began to eat, surprised but not deterred by the hesitancy of the others.

Anna turned and walked away to greet a middle-aged couple who had seated themselves at a nearby table.

When she returned to the couple's table bearing drinks, Sybil attracted Anna's attention.

"Miss, these orders are wrong."

"Three of them are wrong, Anna," Cheville clarified, "Caleb's is fine."

From memory, Anna repeated their orders back to them.

The diners nodded in agreement, impressed with the recital.

"That is what I brought you," Anna stated, "minus the substitutions."

Sybil raised her eyebrows questioningly.

"We have no substitutions."

Before Sybil could phrase an adequate retorque, Caleb piped up, his mouth empty but awaiting the forkful of correct cuisine that was halted before it.

"It's just like the sign says, and the menu, and this," plopping one greasy child sized index finger on the small dessert menu card that stood upright in the center of their table.

"No substitutions," he read, to remove any doubt.

He then completed the transit of the fork to his mouth, pleased to have cleared up the confusion. He wondered to himself why adults had such difficulties with focus.

"I've never heard of such an absurd idea. Why.."

"Is it a COVID thing?" Jason asked, not willing to let Caleb take the male lead in this silly drama.

"Oh no sir. Charlie has always operated that way."

"What about 'The customer is always right'?"

"That's' a catchy name, too. A little long, though. Is that the name of a restaurant back where you're from?"

"No," Sybil replied curtly, irritated at the inane question.

"I would not expect so. It would not be profitable now, would it?"

"This is not what we ordered," Cheville repeated.

"No refunds?" Sybil suggested.

"Yes, we have that. But not until next week. Oh boy, news travels quickly. And you are from out of town?"

"If you are still here, you can check back then."

"Are you telling us, no refunds for a week."

"We are leaving today or tomorrow at the latest. Right, Sybil?"

"Yes."

"It's not for a week, but in a week."

Jason had abandoned his character, and begun eating, depositing unwanted parts on Caleb's plate. The boy evaluated each like an overfed pet, taking a few morsels, but ignoring the bulk of the discards.

"We are here only for a short period."

"That is a shame. Charlie has plans for the grand opening."

"Like free food?"

"No," Anna replied, now as confused as the diners.

"That would be kind of crazy. Where are you folks from?"

"Brentville," Sybil answered for the table.

"I've never heard of it. If there is nothing else," she said, dropped the check in front of Sybil, then started to turn away.

"I don't understand any of this," Sybil said firmly.

"No menu substitutions, no refunds for a week."

Anna turned back for a final attempt at explanation.

"No refunds in a week, not for a week, ma'am."

"What's the difference?"

"If no returns becomes as popular for ice cream as no substitutions is for complete meals, it will be open much longer than for a week. Charlie and me will do just fine."

Cheville abandoned the cause and joined Jason and Caleb in eating.

"Thanks for stopping by and enjoy your meals. Make sure and tell your friends in Brentville about No Substitutions and No Refunds."

CHAPTER EIGHTEEN

"Did you pack my clothes this morning, Cheville?"

"Why would she do that Jason?"

"Cheville normally does that."

"No, I don't. I am neither housekeeper nor valet. I made that clear."

"You did it once."

"I've done a lot of things once."

"You could have told me."

"I have, you chose not to listen."

Jason smacked the steering wheel.

"Don't blame my car, dear," Sybil ordered.

"I'm out my best set of clothes. How would you react if someone had tossed your best outfit?"

"Men don't have outfits Jason, unless they are on safari."

"This is near enough."

"Ha," she laughed.

"Men have clothes, and what you left behind."

"Cheville left them."

"She's not a nanny."

"She is a nanny, sort of."

"She isn't your nanny. Do you require one?"

"A nanny? No. I do not require a nanny, not you and not Cheville. I'm sorry."

He took a breath.

"What I need are my clothes returned."

He began looking for a wide spot in the roadway in order to turn around.

"Those clothes should be burned. By this time, hotel housekeeping will have put them in a hazmat bag and scheduled themselves for a booster shot.

We'll get you new clothes in the new town, maybe even an outfit with a safari worthy hat."

It was Cheville's hour for music, and she had selected a station that she knew was among Jason's favorites.

She herself could make no sense of music. It was as if an explosion arrived across a vacuum, flashes of light but no sound sense. She thought herself blind and someone trying to describe the endless varieties of skyscapes.

If you tapped a guitar string with a child's tiny hammer, why did it not sound like a piano?

Let Jason enjoy it.

He was sure they would stop for the day before Cheville's allotted time had expired.

The sun was a few inches from touching the earth as they rolled forward, the road rising to meet the star.

A sign alongside the road announced, "Fresh oil and chips."

"That sounds appetizing," but no one responded to his comment.

Jason enjoyed the cool of the air-conditioned air as it sighed from the vents. The outside air was nearly the same humidity and temperature, mooting its effort. Equally relished was the song now playing, whose length was conducive to thought. It was melancholic, with simple lyrics. November Rain. He glanced out the left side window. The music clashed with the clear, dry, June evening. It was a perfect offset.

He had become accustomed to the slower pace mandated by his aunt. It was peculiar; he had dreamt of a long voyage with no particular destination, but he not envisioned undertaking it in his aunt's minivan, with her beside him, and Cheville and Caleb in along for the ride.

The Denvers of the world could wait.

He had asked Caleb to search for more remote roads and to plot them. Jason had suggested, through the ruse of a complaint, the results to Sybil and she had agreed to follow the obscure routes. He could ramble along this way forever he mused, with nary an irritated driver behind him.

Jason leaned back, his head against the leather rest. His gaze slid slowly from left to right, and then back again, as Jason enjoyed the sights that he had the time to savor.

"Can you smell the roses?" Sybil asked.

"Not with the windows up."

"They are sweeter than freeway diesel."

Jason pressed a button and the driver's side window lowered. A moment later, he sneezed, and instantly raised the window.

"Ragweed, not roses," he said, and sneezed again.

A few minutes later, a motorcycle overtook them on the narrow road, passing quickly but oddly quietly as it too ascended toward the top of the ridge.

Jason would have overtaken more quickly or not at all, if he had been astride the bike.

The driver was young, bearded, his arms raised as his hands grips the elevated bar of the motorcycle.

He was nonchalant, as relaxed as Jason had been a moment earlier.

"This could be bad," Jason whispered, as he eased his foot from the accelerator, and rapidly evaluated the width of the country road's shoulder.

The motorcyclist eased back into the right lane, and Jason exhaled.

Sybil looked up and saw the rider before them, silhouetted, highlighted by red daytime taillights, a man on a stylized cross, leading or fleeing them.

"He could have been killed," Cheville said.

"Yes, he could. Anyway, we are nearly there," Sybil replied.

They would have been, but the recent event had distracted Jason and they found themselves on the Pennsylvania turnpike.

"At least we are going in the correct direction," Cheville said soothingly.

"It won't kill us to exceed forty miles per hour until the first exit. We can then resume our glacial pace," Jason said.

"Don't look at me like that, Aunt Sybil. It was an accident."

"That is what I'm afraid of. How many more accidents should I expect?"

"None."

"Other than this one? You've already exceeded none."

"You didn't expect it, did you?"

"No."

"So, you should not expect any more. He tried to joke, I feel like I'm retaking my driver's test, knowing in advance that you will fail me, regardless of how I perform."

"That's life, Jason."

"Do you hear that, Caleb? This is life. Accidents abound. If we reach seventy miles per hour we may jump back in time."

"I wish we could."

Cheville hoped that Sybil wanted to talk about the past, to share her past, but she was disappointed. Sybil only wanted to complain, and now that Jason had acknowledged his error, and they were exiting the tollway, she had no fresh topic that was satisfactorily annoying.

"I didn't realize what the country had become when we started this trip. Fluoridated water was the least of our worries. Its electronics attached to our bodies that are the actual threat.

Smart phones should be banned, their suppression would be in the best tradition of America. These devices sap our intelligence, and frankly we don't have much to squander.

They are marketed as an aid, a private nurse, but in my opinion, they are a crutch that inevitability morphs into a dependency, and soon afterward, an addiction that makes of us permanent cripples."

143

"So, you don't like them?"

Sybil frowned and then glanced at Cheville.

"Cheville is the sensible one."

"How's that?"

"I see that you have one of those things, but you're not fondling it every twenty seconds like a fetish worry bead. I've never seen you use it. I call that sensible. It's for emergencies."

Sybil had run out of steam and was silent for a few minutes.

"It's good that you were able to find an exit so quickly, Jason."

"Why?"

"I had the vehicle adjusted so it won't go over fifty-five. We'd have been run over for sure."

CHAPTER NINETEEN

Sybil had second thoughts about quitting the high-speed route. It would soon be dark and they had no reservations for the night. She had not wanted to commit. The further they got from Brentville, the more her uncertainty grew.

There is a point in every trip, where you can begin to sense the destination. It's somewhere between real and virtual. It's the worst part of the trip.

Jason had asked her where they were going, and the truth was she had no answer.

To calm her anxiety, she spoke.

"If we'd done this trip in winter, we'd have seen none of what we've seen.

Every day is special. Had we started yesterday or tomorrow we would have missed this today."

It was inane, but no one critiqued her statement.

Jason, alert for hotel signs, sensed that his life, like this unique day of his aunt's, was slipping away, while simultaneously pressure was mounting, to conform, to find a permanent job and home, to pick up the slack that others regarded as beneath them. "Or was it beyond them?" he wondered.

An image of cowboys came to mind, but he quickly dismissed it as childish.

Hannah's funeral was in Sybil's thoughts. If it could happen so suddenly to an eighteen year old in perfect health....a silly accident, a trip down stairs and then extinguishment. What chance had she? Zero.

A few more years if she was lucky. It was late, but time remained for a change. A change was not an improvement, cautioned her inner voice for the uncounted time.

Time, time, time. It rolled by like the miles on the odometer. "Is that why she limited their miles per day? What difference did it make?

Cheville sat silently, contemplating this role that she had never auditioned for, and for which she seemed sentenced to act as a permanent understudy for the vanished star.

How had she permitted this happen, she asked herself in her few moments off stage. The troupe consisted of virtual strangers.

She was not anxious for a big break; any break would suffice. As to the director...

Ironically, Sybil's thoughts were running on parallel tracks.

People refused to comply with her vision. She envied movie directors. The local theater director in Brentville had more power than she did over these recalcitrant actors. But tomorrow would be a new day.

Caleb was enjoying the trip immensely. The van itself was an air-conditioned cocoon that they left periodically for successive events that seem to exceed each other in offering amusement and entertainment. He could do this forever. Maybe he really could remain nine years old.

Just when Sybil was concerned that they might have to camp overnight in the Odyssey, just when she accepted that it might in fact be cursed, as Cheville had alleged, a vacancy sign appeared out of the light mist. It was one of those old-time campground motels from seventy years ago.

"A little older than me," she thought, as Jason pulled into an open spot before the office.

CHAPTER TWENTY

It was a cool morning. Sybil shivered slightly as she sat.

The car stalled as Jason went to put it in gear

"How long have you had this car?"

"Why? It's in excellent condition. I just don't drive it much. It's more of a"

"A trophy. I heard

If you drove it more, you'd know the difference between the start button, this," he indicated, pushing it softly. The engine sprang to life. "And that," he said, pressing another button, "is the passenger heater seat."

"Thanks," she said.

Sybil closed her eyes, weary of mechanized motion. Perhaps she would buy ear plugs the next time they halted. She wanted more than a diversion, she wanted an escape, quiet and serenity for a while, an indeterminate while, and yet with a dash of adventure. Her unexpected crew was equipped for just the opposite, commotion and misadventure.

She reached over and pressed the stop button.

"Since we can manage 20 miles in a mint condition minivan, we can manage to do some exercise ourselves."

They walked along a wide, well-marked trail, breaking and reforming conversational groups and pairs at random.

While they were all together, Sybil became philosophical.

"We are three generations here. Three species really, like salmon or butterflies, each confident in the permanence of our transitory existence."

"I wish I had eyes like a fly."

"A fly?"

"I could see so much more. And remember even more."

"Believe me Caleb, be grateful for the little you have. Most of life is not worth seeing or committing to memory. A short, good life, well that is an unappreciated gift."

"That's horrible."

"I'm certain that a fly might say the same about our lifespan."

The males walked ahead, leaving the women to talk.

"It's peaceful."

"That's the point."

"It could almost be real life."

"I suppose that for some it is."

"I see that they are looking to hire someone." Sybil nodded.

"Starbucks is hiring. The entire country is hiring and quitting simultaneously. Every grocery store, restaurant, hotel is short of workers. Even the help wanted sign factory can't find enough staff."

Sybil murmured her assent.

"I appear to have a prospective boss in every port."

"What sort of job?" Sybil asked a moment later, worry unmistakable in her voice.

"Or was it relief?" Sybil questioned herself after a few seconds."

"It doesn't matter. I haven't taken it."

"Have you not taken it?"

"That was quick."

"They scan your driver's license, you sign a waiver, and poof, the background check is done, your life evaluated in less time than it takes to pour a flat white. It's incredible, the speed. Its faster than Saint Peter. You know, that sounds like a really depressing job, right hand man on Earth, and now a celestial bouncer."

They continued to walk along in silence for a few minutes.

"Really, Starbucks?"

It took a moment for Cheville to recognize that the conversation had come back to her. She had come to appreciate the serenity of being taken for granted when she wasn't being ignored. It provided her with time to reflect.

Cheville continued to stare at the scenery, then her eyes returned to rest on those of Sybil. The older woman was expecting a response.

"No. It was a job in a bank. Some regional manager was staying at the hotel, and he must have liked what he saw."

"I bet he did, Cheville."

"You should have done your own background check. On him. Instead, I imagine that you just handed over your driver's license."

"If I'd done that, I'd have failed. Give me some credit. I've been around the block, not as often as you, you are a regular Le Mans in more ways than one. We went to the bank first, in a back office."

"I've been there, done that, repeatedly."

"Why did you turn down the job?"

"I don't know. A better question would be why did I take it? If I had that is."

"Was he handsome?"

"What does that have to do with anything?"

"For me, it sometimes has to do with everything."

"I guess so" Cheville said, Sybil unsure if the response was to her question, or commentary on her most recent phrase.

"I might be available for a temporary position, or several, if I find it satisfying."

"I see."

"Let's drop this topic. It's not the first time that I've been approached during this exciting trip. Typically, Caleb is my inoculation as his presence keeps them at bay."

"They?"

"Viruses, solitary lions, men. You know this, Sybil. Why ask the obvious?"

"I'm bored."

Several moments later, Cheville returned to the topic.
"

I'm worried what impact that would have on Caleb."

"And on Jason?"

"He's moody. His reaction wouldn't last."

"Ask him."

"Jason?"

"You know him as well as I do. Ask Caleb."

"Who said anything about Caleb?"

Cheville's voice was so serious that Sybil laughed.

"I have asked him."

"You have?"

"Indirectly. You are not seeing the normal Caleb."

"Oh?"

"This trip is fun, for him," Cheville qualified.

"And for you?"

Cheville ignored the question, her lack of a response shouted 'No'.

"We move so much; I do that is. I bring him along in his opinion. He is moved as much as one would move furniture."

Cheville stopped.

"He is ecstatic."

"He is?" Sybil asked, surprised at the disappointment in her own voice.

"He would be. I know Caleb better than anyone."

"That's normal."

"Is it? He would see it as a way to start over. It would be a decision in which he for once had some say. Sybil, the logistics would be overwhelming."

"Life is overwhelming."

"Modern life especially. It's not the eighteenth century, when you could just pull into a new town and just start over."

"It wasn't that simple even then."

"It wasn't?"

"I have no personal experience," Sybil said, smiling, "but transitions are difficult. Don't let paperwork hold you back, it's the two-dimensional version of naysayers."

"The first time it happened, I found it odd that I was approached about a job. It's crazy, but I truly thought they were talking about something for Caleb. Isn't that ridiculous?"

Sybil nodded in agreement.

"He's much too young. Anyway, the job offer was for me. You know how things are today, jobs are everywhere, and prospective employees are on long term vacation. No one is willing to be hired."

"Including you."

They reached a point where Sybil decided that they should turn around.

"Already?" Jason asked.

The boy had already turned back toward the campground.

"Yes, it's time. See, Caleb agrees. Caleb is not a whiner, not like that spoiled brat, the constant complainer in Brentville."

Jason thought back to the day that he had retrieved the van, readying it for the trip. Sybil mentioned the inhabitants of Brentville as if each and every one of them was a cast member on a well-known, long running television program.

"Too much competition for you, Aunt Sybil?"

"Fortunately, his grandfather died quickly, and he and his mother left town shortly after the funeral."

"I missed that episode," he joked.

"As I expected. It was obvious that they did not care about the grandfather.

I don't know what I'd have done if the old man had lasted a few more weeks.

You three would be on this wonderful trip alone.

You're lucky he died when he did."

Cheville and Jason glanced at each other. What was she talking about?

"Before I decided to take the odyssey, I considered thumbing rides."

"You didn't?"

"I certainly did."

"It's not safe."

"Nothing is safe at my age."

"Can we attend a pro basketball game?" Caleb asked.

"What makes you ask that, Caleb?"

"I want to see if it's more entertaining than what's televised."

"Such as what?"

"They show grown men running around, throwing a ball into a net. It looks so simple that there must be more at the arena itself."

"Nope," Cheville answered.

"No, unless you count the cheerleaders," Jason said.

"Why do people go then? The game is so boring."

"That's the idea I think," Sybil ventured.

"No, it isn't," Jason argued.

"What is the idea of sports?"

"It's not that."

"The kids I know are bored with basketball after 10 minutes. It's the same thing over and over."

"I like video games," Caleb exclaimed.

Cheville sensing that the moment was ripe, with her curiosity overcoming courtesy, asked

"You never had children?"

"I was never much for children. I suppose I can say that safely now as a retired teacher."

"Did you never want any?"

"I had a few."

Sybil smiled at their shocked faces.

"Boys," she added.

"My third and fourth husbands, they were children, but talented ones."

She winked at Cheville.

"A few semiserious companions along the way, men in most ways, but boys in temperament. It's like the tropics; beautiful weather and gorgeous weather, but there are no long days like in the higher latitudes. You can't have it all, but most is enough."

"Oh, they're necessary. Authentic boys that is. My career depended on their continuous delivery. I had them forty hours per week and that was sufficient."

"Did any of them stand out?"

"Yes, some for the wrong reasons."

She paused for a moment, long enough that Cheville was prepared to change the subject.

"I remember three of my boys, students of mine I mean. I was never fool enough to actually raise any of my own. These were three of the best, yet they killed themselves drunk driving.

They hit the same tree, spun on ice and crashed through a chain link fence and hit the tree. Irony of ironies the fence surrounded, and the tree stood within the very cemetery in which they would be buried a few days later."

"How terrible. One accident claimed three of your students."

"I wish that were true. But no, it was three separate accidents, spread over 5-10 years, with death, it doesn't make sense to mark time. It's the end of time. Stupid. So smart and so stupid. They say that only the good die young, but the intelligent don't seem far behind."

Sybil had enough closets of skeletons that she had no compunction about asking those of others. She wouldn't share hers, but she enjoyed comparing her collection with theirs.

The admonition about casting stones took half the fun from life. Hypocrisy was hilarity and was surely meant to be part of tolerant American life.

"I taught enough history to conclude that we should not teach history, except maybe a few highlights. I remember old family reunions where skeletons were left buried. But there was one cousin who couldn't leave a spade a spade, propped inconspicuously in the toolshed. He had to dig up past indiscretions and reintroduce them to attendees, especially the new arrivals. He'd have made a

157

wonderful historian. And now, with ancestry and 23 and alone..."

Jason cocked his head at the malapropism but did not correct his aunt.

"History is counterproductive. It provides no actionable guidance. We no longer attempt to use it as intended, as a spade to bury the dead, but instead as a weapon to exhume the putrid bodies and revitalize their mistakes and hatreds as our own. The spite endures. It's worse than sports."

"Wow, so I guess I won't be listening to the history of sports today when it's my turn later today."

"I'm simply saying that the past of dead strangers is not yours to relive."

"What happened to your cousin?"

"The busybody?"

"Yes, the busybody," Caleb echoed, relishing the chance to use such a funny word.

"I don't know. I stopped attending reunions."

Cheville asked Jason to walk with her, and she had soon established a lead far enough ahead to conduct a private discussion.

"Any complaints?" Cheville asked.

He shrugged

"You?"

"I have a list as long as Sybil's stack of complaints is high as to why I have none of my own."

"Tell me."

"Number one, Sybil is paying for this trip."

"So are you," his astuteness disconcerting.

"Caleb is enjoying it. He is learning so much, so many new things."

"Some good, some not so good."

Cheville nodded in agreement.

"Overall, its good."

She took a deep breath before adding,

"Learning not good can be good."

It was Jason's turn to agree with a nod of his head.

"What else?" he asked.

"This trip makes me thinks, no, it lets me think. It's like pressure, I can't describe which pressure, but pressure has been relieved. For a while," she said regretfully.

"You have pressure?" Jason joked, then abruptly stopped speaking.

"What else?"

Cheville smiled, any future reappearance of pressure temporarily forgotten.

"I'm able to spend more time with you than ever before."

She looked away and then back directly in his eyes.

"Despite it not being voluntary on your part."

"I'm here, aren't I?'

"For your aunt. She invited us, you did not."

Jason did not correct her. It was too late and too difficult to explain.

"And because you have nothing better to do."

"That makes two of us," he said angrily.

"Here's to a free ride," Cheville replied, raising an imaginary glass.

"I see now that our two families are perfectly matched in bizarreness. In a weird way I find it comfortable."

"What else?"

"I've always wanted to see Ohio.'

He laughed.

"How long do you want this to last?"

"I don't know, Cheville."

"What else?" Jason asked after a long silence.

"She's sick."

"Who's sick?"

"Sybil. Who else?"

"How do you know Sybil is sick? Did she tell you? How sick? You must be wrong. Sybil has never been sick."

"How would you know? Oh, never mind, Jason. Forget that I said anything"

"Forgotten."

But it was not forgotten.

"If Sybil is sick Cheville, it doesn't change anything."

"It's only about Sybil. I don't understand why she invited us along. I didn't before, but now I think I do. She required someone to complain about and to. That is my role. Me and Caleb's assigned parts."

"What else?"

"There is nothing else. I wasn't kidding about wanting to see Ohio."

They reached the van, and mounted aboard, each in his assigned spot-on stage.

It was Caleb's music hour, and his first selection was a talk radio call- in program.

After several minutes, Jason joked,

"These callers excel at complainers. This show should be sponsored by a cheese company."

Always men on talk radio.

Not to be outdone, Sybil critiqued the moaners and the complainers.

Her adult companions prayed that the station would not find its place among Sybil's favorites.

Caleb enjoyed the hour immensely, not asking for one switch during his sixty minutes.

The topics were varied but had at their base a shared pessimism.

The callers had nothing but fear, soured with hatred. Hatred in lieu of tolerance and reasoned compromise.

Fear of the future, fear of the past, fear of the present. Fear crushing optimism.

A twenty-year veteran of the air force questioned aloud whether the country remained worth defending.

Buying guns and gold as if one was planning a catastrophic picnic.

There was no consensus on where the country should go, or how to get there.

It was an AA meeting where despair was the required dress.

Covid will pass, climate change may replace the virus' position center stage. The waters may rise, covering land that used to be America

Stock trading central bankers and trial judges have joined the cadre of corrupt career politicians

"Men have no imagination," Sybil said in disgust.

"We can fix this, easily. Men are such wimps today. You," she said, assigning Jason all responsibility of his gender.

"Just look at all the repetitive games and gods you've dreamt up. Any professor of creativity would fail them and eject them from class. You're hopeless."

Jason could not prevent himself from laughing.

"I've made it from chauffeur to ruler of the planet in three phone calls."

"Not after me the deluge, the flood is now," Sybil added.

The final caller of the hour offered his proof on Covid.

"It's like this Covid. Of course it is manmade, just look at what the governments do and pay no attention to what they said. They never acted this way before. We can't handle the truth, so it's not offered to us."

Sybil snorted, the sound providing Caleb with no small amount of amusement.

"And here I was naïve to believe that one had to sign on to the internet to find more people to dislike."

"I know the feeling," Cheville said quietly.

"The fact is that people act on myth. Facts are for foolish opinion writers who have sentences but no convictions.

We are more likely to die in a car crash than from Covid," Cheville offered.

"Yeah, I guess we are," Jason replied.

"This van has great crash test results," Caleb added.

"Jason wasn't the driver in those tests."

"Well, we stick to back roads and daytime driving."

"You have your family to consider."

"What do you mean family? You?

You're close to your expiration date. Let's be honest."

"Ok. I'll be honest. I didn't mean me."

Jason blushed.

"I'm glad to be in charge."

"In charge?" She said, her voice between tease and mockery.

"Only fools want to be in charge, to own the so-called world. Fools convince themselves of ridiculous ideas. I'm content as passenger. It relieves me of understanding the owner's manual."

"But you're setting the course."

"This is one car, not the world. Pay attention to the road."

"As for the rest of the world, it is in the hands of those who..."

"Those who step up?"

"Yes, Sybil agreed before suddenly bursting into laughter. It was serious laughter, uncontrolled and of long duration. It came in waves that subsided and then appeared again, like a respawned character.

"Those who step up," she repeated once, eliciting from herself another series of guffaws.

"Me, I prefer to step out."

Sybil leaned back and closed her eyes, signaling that the conversation was over.

CHAPTER TWENTY-ONE

They had passed a late 19th century barn that was slowly undressing itself at the insistence of time and the elements. It was degrading and depressing, as if one could feel embarrassed on her behalf.

The decrepitude was matched by an equally malignant urban blight, in this case a small village where entire streets of homes were victims of a wood devouring fungi with an insatiable appetite.

"Are you sure this is the right place?"

"You should understand by now that there is no right place," Cheville said, exasperated.

"It's a place."

"More or less."

"If we were here thirty years ago, one would have said that this town had seen better days. Since then, no days have dawned here."

"It was once a wonderful community. Places and people change one another I suppose."

"Do you remember it?"

"Bits and pieces."

The once cheerful, precisely crowned yellow brick alleys they she recalled were patched in numerous sections with black asphalt, giving the length of walkway the look of a jaundiced arm, covered in dried scabs.

Signs of defunct beer brands hung from the corners of closed family grills, ignored by locals and TV scavenger show teams. Schools, businesses, churches, closed, auctioned or arsoned off. The town was flat but petite, too small to have granted precious level ground to the dead. These latter were likely in hindsight grateful for having been slighted and interred elsewhere.

"Are we staying here?" Caleb asked, dread in his young voice.

"No, Caleb, this is just a short drive by", the term causing the three others to cast their eyes around nervously.

Sybil was unaware of the impact of her words. "There is no place here."

Jason and Sybil walked through the small town, while Caleb and Cheville elected to remain in the van, doors locked.

"Why did you bring us here?"

"They used to have very good ice cream."

Jason's face showed skepticism.

"Does this trip have a purpose? I don't see it if there is one. Cheville has expressed the same sentiment."

"About you? I agree that you don't shout purpose. You should listen to Cheville."

"I'm referring to this trip. Your trip.

"I appreciate being the object of sentiment. But you mustn't listen to Cheville."

"I repeat, don't listen to her. What does she know? About me, or this trip of ours? You invited her along, she accepted, not knowing anything. She doesn't know herself is my observation. She obviously failed sex education and from what I understand, they teach that to kids before they learn

166

their colors. They dumb that down like most curriculum to the level of sheep. She made the cut."

"You're being cruel. You know what I mean."

"People say that when they have no argument and want us to accept their misperceptions as being beyond reproach. If I know what you mean, there is no need for a discussion."

"Whatever."

"Cruelty becomes you, but really Aunt Sybil, sheep?"

There are two types of people; those who do and those who teach. And then there are few of us"

"That makes three."

"Don't interrupt. A few of us complain and push the world forward."

Sybil looked around at the bleak surroundings.

"If you think I'm searching for an escape, you would be wrong."

"There is none," she thought. She had relearned that lesson from the Smith woman. No, she simply desired confirmation that her life had been, if not worthwhile in itself, in support of a worthwhile world. That it had not been, as she had begun to suspect, a decades long practical joke, of which she was the butt.

"Tell me Jason; what do you think should be the goal of our trip

Our trip? When you phrase it that way, simple."

"Abandoning you," he wanted to fire back

"Face the past so you realize that the future won't be much different," he said.

"A final hurrah."

"You're easily distracted, Jason. Does Cheville fall into that category?"

"A distraction? I'm not sure," he replied a few moments later.

"Maybe that's why you have no goals yourself."

"Or it runs in the family and it's not my fault."

"Not your fault, not your merit. It's better to accept too much fault than none at all."

"Did you read that on a recent billboard? I thought those sorts of pithy signs were long out of fashion."

"I appreciate that you are paying the bills. That isn't the type of contribution I'm referring to. It's the route, the destination, the sights we stop for, any decision, large or small, we have no input."

"You're not going to bring that up again."

It was a command not a request.

"What?" he asked, confused

"Road trips are one-way, fresh laundry is not a consideration. This is not some male fantasy road trip movie. The sooner you accept that, the sooner you will appreciate clean clothes. Its effective, if late preparation for the rest of your life.

Small goals ease the pain of large disappointments."

They passed closed stores, abandoned homes, a dozen inhabitants remaining before it qualified as a ghost town.

"I lie now and again. It's wise to stay in shape.

But I ask you this, wanting an honest answer.

168

If you continue to mock the entire itinerary
of this trip, ridiculing each and every stop, up to an
including the sights, the food, well what is the point?"

"Tell me."

"I'm trying to show you, to let you see life
without worrying about the petty demands of food
and shelter. Who wants to be a hermit?"

"Of course not.".

"This used to be a beautiful town, complete,
a whole unto itself. Its life is gone. Art, vanished.

Art, be it music or literature or painting. I
think that it is like diamonds or gold, not actually
created by the artist."

"No?"

"I think not, they, the artists that is, are
happily deluded. Delusion is reality. But that's
another theory."

"Or delusion."

"Art is discovered, not created."

"Just like diamonds or gold."

"Yes. Lying there or floating by, open to be
grasped by a lucky one. Like your lottery, you see?"

Jason perked up at the talk of lottery tickets,
as he bought one nearly every day.

"They sell tickets in advance, buying a week's
worth would be simpler."

"And less fun. I admit that I need the fix.

This is a dream," he said, holding a crumpled
one he pulled from his front pants pocket, the spot
where men keep precious items, and held it aloft like
a host at Christian mass.

"It's less money than an eight ball or a
highball, without a hangover. Six little white balls,

each a component of heaven, mixed together to create a lifetime of bliss."

He exhaled the remnant of air still in his lungs.

He inhaled slightly before adding,

"What's not to like?"

"Look around Jason, there are none for sale here."

She turned back to where Cheville and Caleb waited.

"Leave our debris here."

They walked back to the Odyssey, empty handed.

They were stopped underneath the freeway, waiting for the light to change. In the left turn lane next to them, a young man sat aside his coughing motorcycle, its bass offset the high tones of Alicia Keys' Girl on Fire. The music filled the car, its satellite signal undeterred by the layer of concrete that overhung the vehicle

"It's repetitive," Sybil remarked.

"Turn it off," Jason and Cheville commanded in unison.

"This is your sort of music," Sybil commented while reducing the volume to where the song was inaudible.

"It was once. My sister liked that song."

"Did she outgrow it?"

"I suppose that she did in a way."

Sybil nodded knowingly

"What does she listen to now?"

170

"Not that I care," she told herself.

"I'm not sure. I'll ask her the next chance we meet."

"You're not close?"

"We used to be."

"I see. Things change. And so do redlights. Its green, Jason."

Both he and the motorcyclist were equally lost in the thoughts that young men have, Sybil concluded. It's difficult for them to stay on task.

Driving is a hunt; it consumes all of their concentration. Once they stop at a redlight, or pause for another reason, they nearly collapse from exhaustion. Or so, Sybil had experienced.

My Fair Lady had it wrong she believed

"Why can't a man be more like a woman?" she said aloud.

"Is that a song?" Jason asked.

"It's not very popular," Sybil replied.

As the Odyssey lurched forward, and the motorcyclist veered left up the freeway ramp, Sybil pressed a radio button at random and adjusted the volume upwards.

Another unfamiliar tune began to play midstream

"They make the best lovers."

"Who does?"

"Never mind.

That is how life happens. Chance encounters occur midstream, which we mistake for a beginning.

Was this trip the same? Despite her planning, or what passed for planning, really it had been a sketch, and it remained little more than a few shaded lines. The trip had begun long before the idea had sprouted in her mind. The Odyssey was packed with four travelers, each filled with their own desires, and fears, and best and worst of all, secrets. They were there, as hidden as the miscellany that lay undisturbed in the crevasses of the leather seats.

And the trip would end in the conventional sense that trips end. But it would continue, as each of them spun off in different directions like dislodged hubcaps.

Jason looked in the rear-view mirror to verify that the rear occupants were wearing headphones.

Satisfied, he spoke.

"Cheville's sister is dead."

"I know.

I can read between the lines. Backward or forward, it makes no difference.

I've gone through the seven stages of death so often that it has become a well-rehearsed dance step. I can breeze through it in triple time, unaware that I've completed the routine in less time than it requires to brew a pot of coffee.

When I hear of something dreadful that has happened to an acquaintance or a distant friend, I dream up what I can do to help them. It can be a new car or a full ride scholarship for a surviving child."

"That's wonderful. How did I never hear of this?"?

"Sorry to be blunt, but you don't strike me as the anonymous donor type."

"What was your most recent donation, Aunt Sybil?

Not me, obviously."

"What about this road trip?"

"Yes, there is this road trip."

"Tell me about the others. I'm amazed at this sudden switch in your behavior."

"It isn't."

"You've done this for a while. You must be better off than that Linda Smith woman Jason has told me about. Who benefited from your largess?"

"It isn't behavior."

"What?"

"It's a dream, a way to make me feel good. I pretend that I help them, and it helps me. I have the benefit at zero cost. Like Caleb and his internet world. It doesn't have to be real to be real good. A placebo, you might say. No Wi-Fi needed."

After a long moment of shocked silence, Jason quipped, "At least we got a road trip, Cheville. That's a dream in and of itself."

"And coffee."

"Which reminds me..."

"You want to stop for coffee."

"I need to stop because of coffee."

"It needs to exit. The coffee. That's the eighth stage by the way."

"The eighth stage of what?"

"Of dealing with death, of course. We aren't discussing caffeine.

The eighth stage is our own exit.

Here, just up there is a good spot.

Pullover.

Time for ice cream."

The complexity of the order was inversely related to age, with the number of children in line she anticipated a long wait.

"I should have brought my copy of War and Peace."

"Abridged?"

"It wouldn't matter," Sybil replied.

"You have lots of time. You have been reminding us of that fact for over a week. I'd like a banana split with everything he said to the server when it was his turn. Take your time, we are in no hurry."

"Three spoons?"

"No, just one."

Sybil had seen a zoo advertised in one of the flyers found in their hotel.

"We will stop there tomorrow. Don't worry, Caleb.

The zoo is small," she said, directing her comment to Cheville.

"So, the creatures are more obliging, only semi wild, like husbands."

To Caleb, she said assuredly,

"The animals are full sized."

"They won't have everything."

"No one has everything."

"San Diego does."

"I know for a fact that they don't have a zwarg."

"What's that?"

"A sort of Komodo dragon native to a few islands in the north of Japan."

"Well San Diego has more than this zoo will."

"It is a zoo, we are not going on safari, despite Jason's new clothes."

"I know," Caleb replied, not sure what that had to do with the zoo. He was still trying to picture a zwarg.

"If they don't have a particular animal, they might be able to make do.":

"With what?" Jason asked.

"Like in theater."

"Makeup?" asked Cheville helpfully.

"Yes, makeup. And costumes. If they don't have a gorilla, or if the gorilla is sick, or on vacation."

"Gorillas don't get vacation."

"They don't. That sounds very unfair. Gorillas must get vacation. Otherwise there would be no need for gorilla costume for the chimpanzee to wear."

"Unless the zoo has no gorilla."

"That's possible. In which case, they would still have need of a gorilla costume."

"I don't know, that doesn't sound right."

"The same for the zebra wearing the rhinoceros suit."

"A rhinoceros suit?"

"If it is a zebra in a rhinoceros suit, I will let you know Caleb. I can always tell the difference."

"You can?"

"Of course, it's easier if the rhinoceros is wearing a zebra suit."

"It wouldn't fit."

"You would be surprised at what they can do with these new materials. Still, I can tell by my nose. Rhinos have a very distinctive smell."

"How do you know?"

"Sybil has been around quite a few horny pigs, Caleb" Cheville responded.

"She is a regular horn hunter."

"But rhinos are endangered."

"Just like in Brentville," Sybil sighed.

She looked at Cheville.

"There is more to life than food, clean sheets, and a car."

"Add money and what else is required?"

"Love?"

"Love is dessert. I'm on a diet, a restricted diet not of my choosing. What about you?"

"Sugar free. It's not the same."

"You are quiet today, Aunt Sybil."

"Yes," she confirmed.

"No complaints?"

"I'm working on. Don't rush me."

"You enjoy whining. I only wish that you weren't as good as it as you are."

"Practice makes perfect."

"I'd have selected another adjective."

"Caleb."

"He's not perfect."

"He's important..."

"I'm pleased to hear that."

"To you."

"When I was his age, I had already."

"Cover your years Caleb," Jason interjected, but the warning was unnecessary, as the boy had earbuds placed to entertain him. He had taken to wearing his mask again for some unknown reason.

"That is exactly what I mean. He needs to inhabit the real world, not some addictive, for nothing but profit metaverse."

"If you say so."

"We should all say so."

"She said don't rush her, Jason. She's on track now," Cheville cautioned good naturedly.

"At his age, I'd already smoked tobacco."

She glanced in the rear view mirror before adding, "Cigarettes, pipes, even a cigar. All equally nasty I must confess."

"You know," she said almost in an aside to herself, "kids are exposed to everything on the internet but are restricted form doing much in real life, that's IRL Jason, except play sports on the off chance that they will be talented enough to support their parents desire to do everything they, the parents desire IRL.

"Let's stop here for a potty break," she said with a giggle incongruous for her age.

"We just stopped 30 minutes ago."

"That was for us, this is for me."

"Why do you stop so often? You aren't an old man."

"But this is where they'd be likely to stop."

"I'll be back in a few minutes."

"Sybil criticizes me while she sluts through Ohio?"

Caleb had removed his earbuds and overheard Cheville's question.

"Is that like skiing?"

"I suppose it is. She enjoys slaloms."

"What are those?"

"I'm not sure. I've never tried one myself. You can ask Sybil."

"Cheville is teasing you Caleb, there is no skiing in Ohio."

"Don't be so sure, Jason."

Sybil twisted to face Caleb as best she could.

"You can remove your mask now Caleb. The virus has departed."

"I know that."

"Toss it out the window. It will improve the quality of litter in this area. Too many low-end beer cans if you ask me. If it wasn't so useful on this trip, I'd have you dispose of your computer as well. Its trash. Do you agree, Cheville?"

"I defer to your judgment when it comes to trashy items. It's not a bad idea to dump the rubbish at the first opportunity."

"I'm serious, Caleb. That box will rot your mind as thoroughly as sugary drinks will dissolve your teeth and liver."

Sybil turned back to face Jason.

"The pandemic generated this behavior."

"It existed years before Covid."

"It exacerbated the decline. I hate change. It's rarely worth it."

Sybil was satisfied with her sermon and sat back comfortably.

A few minutes later she shocked them all by suggesting that they pull over to let her and Caleb switch seats.

The dashboard clock read 11 :00, prompting Sybil to have Caleb press her preferred preset on the radio. The older woman began to sing along.

"Still, I look to find a reason to believe." A few minutes later, when Sybil's voice trailed off, Cheville asked quietly,

"Does that still work for you?"

"I think so."

"With men?" Cheville pressed on in a cheerful voice.

"Nothing works with men other than the obvious. Men need a reason not to believe, but believe me they don't, or can't, learn."

"You require a lesson too, a skill really, the ability to say no.".

She declined, as she had in all of their conversations, to add, Aunt Sybil.

"A man at every stop, I understand why you are avoiding freeways, they would only impede you."

"I'm being impeded often enough," retorted Sybil, irreproachable.

"Nearly every night, if my estimates are correct. That makes..."

"Not enough. I was never good at math."

"But you taught it for years."

"Exactly."

Cheville spoke.

"Do you find reason to say no?"

Sybil considered the question.

"No."

She laughed.

"Life is too long, too large to fill with no's."

"I was surprised..."

"Surprises can be fun."

"Or disappointing."

"I prefer fun."

"Jason warned me,"

"About me."

Cheville nodded.

"No one warned Jason."

Cheville let the barely veiled insult pass, and then reconsidered her silence.

"He said you were a slu.....g"

"What's a sluuug?" a young male voice demanded from the relished seat in front.

The women noticed that Caleb had closed his computer and was following their high stakes banter. Both were grateful for its extinguishment by the boy's interruption.

"Do you mean a slug? She is anything but a slug. She moves faster than all of us."

"That she does, Caleb."

"Oh good, there is the zoo."

CHAPTER TWENTY-TWO

"Have you seen Sybil?" Jason asked Cheville.

"No."

"She left earlier," Caleb said.

"Alone?"

The boy shrugged, then added, "I think so."

Jason left them and returned a few minutes later.

"The Odyssey is missing as well."

"It can't be missing as it belongs to Sybil."

"I hope that she hasn't done something drastic."

"Of course she has, Jason. The curtain on drastic rose over a week ago. I don't know if today is intermission, or if it's been a one woman one act play the whole time and we are extraneous."

"What could she have possibly done?"

"I can't waste another week speculating. I wish I could say good riddance, that I don't care, but whatever she has done impacts us."

"They could have arrested her," Caleb ventured.

The adults stared at the boy.

"I like Sybil."

"But?"

"People always say later that they liked them."

"Who is them?"

"Serial murderers."

"Caleb!"

"She may be revisiting bloody scenes or scouting her next victims. It could be us."

"If I end up murdered, promise me that you'll brush your teeth, morning and night. I won't be there to remind you," Cheville admonished.

He looked at her

"I'm serious," he said plaintively.

"So am I."

Jason said nothing, only frowned deeply.

"The places we've visited are ideal for hiding a corpse."

"You may be on to her," Cheville added, and then grinned.

"It's preferable to being stuffed in among strangers in a crowded cemetery where all the good views are taken by folks who won't budge.

Lakes, and forests, even abandoned railways, death could be worse."

Caleb retreated from his theory.

"Ok, maybe she was kidnapped."

"I pity the kidnappers. They will be scarred for life. Or longer."

"Longer than life?" Jason retorted.

"Sybil clings to the soul, like wood smoke in hair."

She sniffed Caleb.

"That reminds me. Go take another shower. It may be your last for a while."

The boy headed toward their room.

"The good news is that we'll enjoy a warm hotel room and a clean meal, until Sybil returns. Or is it the other way round?"

"And what do we do in the interim? Wrinkle like a peach undisturbed on a kitchen counter?"

"Always the poet."

"I don't appreciate sarcasm,".

"It is not sarcasm. I intended it as a compliment."

"Sorry. Thank you.".

"She may remind you of one, but she doesn't strike me as an untouched peach."

The conversation ended as Sybil entered the hotel from the parking lot.

"Where have you been?" Jason demanded.

"Caleb thought that you were arrested or kidnapped."

"It was nearly as terrible. I went to church."

"Church?" Jason exclaimed.

"We left little Rome in order to attend services here?"

"I didn't see you there Jason."

"That's a simple answer to a simple question. It may disappoint Caleb."

"Church?" Jason repeated.

"You are going to break his heart," Cheville commented.

"It will do him good. He needs his heart broken at some time. We all do."

"I suppose that in your world it builds character."

"We're all of us in the same world. I doubt that a broken heart improves character. It builds empathy."

She paused.

"Caleb's character is fine. You have done well."

183

Cheville was silenced by the rare
compliment, leaving Jason to once again bleat,
"Church?"
"I like to go for the tips."
"Really? Like don't be bad."
"It's not having any impact, Sybil."
"Fashion tips."
"Seriously?"
"You go to church for fashion tips?"
"It's not necessary to attend every week.
Once per season is sufficient. Easter is the best."
"This is the height of summer."
"I see your point. And you are right, the tips
weren't very good."

"I think that you will enjoy our next stop. No
Jason, not that type of stop."
"Is it a surprise?"
"We are staying in Lebanon for a few days."
"What's there?"
"Oh, all types of things; theater, antiques,
trains, the Golden Lamb."
"Skiing?" Caleb asked.
"I don't think so, maybe, who knows?", Sybil
replied, perplexed to see Cheville blush when Caleb
exclaimed,
"Great. Slaloms sound like fun."

"I had to look it up the other day on the hotel
computer," she said when none of her companions
offered encouragement for the upcoming stop.

"I pictured it as some new age church, one that would find no followers In Brentville, except maybe Mike Hayes, but even his craziness is in remission since he started his tour business."

"How is it doing?", Jason asked, surprised at his own curiosity about someone he did not know.

"Well enough," Sybil replied.

"The golden lamb? That sounds like something from the Old Testament," Cheville remarked.

"What's that?" the boy queried

"It's a restaurant," the nephew answered

"I suppose. Am I correct, Aunt Sybil?"

"A restaurant and a hotel. The Golden Lamb is the oldest hotel in the state of Ohio".

"Oh, ok. But what is the Old Testament? Is it a cookbook?"

The three adults laughed but provided no answer.

The child returned to looking out the window.

Finally, Sybil said, "Yes, Caleb, in a way I suppose it is a cookbook."

Sybil was pleased that the boy had removed the mask. She saw one of its straps projecting from the rubbish bag hanging from the dash.

"You don't look like a stranger now, Caleb."

"Are we strangers?" he asked, his voice full of uncertainty.

"Strangers resemble each other through happenstance and then more so through prolonged contact."

He did not understand the answer, but then she wasn't sure that she did either.

"That is how tribes form."

"Cool."

A pause.

"Are we a tribe?" came the voice from the unaccustomed front of the Odyssey.

It was mildly annoying, this periodic high-pitched question coming as if from the heavens. Still, Sybil smiled at the idea of constructing her own private tribe.

"We are savages, Caleb. That's a start," Jason said confidently.

"This van is beginning to resemble a gypsy wagon," Sybil noted.

"That's racist Aunt Sybil."

"The entire world is racist, Caleb. Get used to. Europe is filled with tribes, the same as Africa. They choose sides and kill each other, then remix the teams and kill each other some more. Sometimes they have interleague play. Its fantasy football played as a deadly game during a never-ending recess for the juvenile minded.

But it's much better here in the land of one tribe. Still, we need to do laundry soon."

As they pulled into the hotel parking lot, Sybil noticed the middle-aged man exiting a car, before she noticed the vehicle itself.

Jason on the other hand, remarked on the sleekness of the car, a brand-new corvette, in what every male under 70 called candy apple red.

"Very nice," he said, eliciting agreement from his aunt.

"Its motion in poetry."

"That's a weird license plate," Cheville commented, "what does it mean?"

"And he is parking in the handicapped section," she added.

"He has a valid sticker," Sybil said, her eyes darting to the car's rear view mirror, before returning their gaze to the stranger.

It was incongruous; a new, convertible corvette with a handicapped parking placard hanging from the rear-view mirror. The personalized license plate exclaimed NT DED YT

"Not dead yet," offered Caleb.

"That must be a sign," Cheville joked.

Their rooms were on the third floor, and there was no elevator.

In twenty years, Sybil imagined that she would not dare attempt this staircase. She thought again of the Smith woman in Brentville, and of her staircase.

"Its good practice for Caleb," Sybil commented.

"Practice for what? I've been climbing stairs for weeks now. And descending them. I don't need the practice."

"For your tennis match tomorrow."

Caleb looked at her with large eyes, then ran up the stairs, neglecting to ask for either the room number or the key.

Many of the doors to the rooms named after American presidents were open, as they served as exhibits when not functioning as normal hotel rooms.

Black plastic chains were strung across the opened door of every unoccupied guest room, inviting visitors to view the museum like setting.

The lack of an elevator and lingering Covid related staff shortages were the only drawbacks.

Restaurants were still unwillingly modeling themselves on 'No Substitutions', but this particular establishment was performing many that most. It had not survived for two centuries being inattentive to its clientele.

"We can rent rackets and used tennis balls."
"It's almost as simple as renting a family, except here you need to provide a deposit."

The keeper of the court returned with the rackets and balls, and the four debutantes ventured into the world of tennis. In the adjacent court, four women were playing.

The skin of one was a darkish yellow from too much sun, genuine and artificial, to the point that, from below the neck, she resembled her Asian companion.

Only Sybil and Caleb were familiar with the rules and scoring in tennis. Familiar in the sense that both rules and scoring undoubtedly existed, but unsure of what these rules and scores may actually be, it was permitted for them to create them on the fly.

Sybil deferred to Caleb's youthful competitiveness and skill compensating energy to assist her as they played as a team. His keener eyesight was an additional plus.

"These yellow balls don't bounce as well as the white ones of my youth. It's the weight of the dye you see. Its simple physics."

"Which subjects did you teach in school, Sybil?"

"Whichever the children needed."

At one point, Jason asked,

"Are we too young for pickle ball?".

"I'm old enough to be your mother, and I am too young to take up pickle ball. Keep playing. It's not like your video games, is it Caleb?" Sybil staccatoed between breaths.

"This is harder than I thought," he managed to pant.

"Less sitting on your ass, and more stepping on the grass," she gasped in response.

"Not even kids can move at the speed of a joystick," Jason reflected.

"Watching others play sportsball is as juvenile as playing it for a career."

"But this is fun," she was able to state before requesting that they pause for a few minutes of rest.

"You're going to be sore tomorrow," Jason warned but it was all four who were stiff the following morning, old and young muscles suffering identically through lack of use. They decided to postpone a rematch to another day, leaving Cheville and Jason free to explore the town, while Sybil and Caleb rejuvenated their tired, bookend bodies.

CHAPTER TWENTY-THREE

The radio in the bar was playing 70s music, which is to say music for 70 year olds. Cheville glanced in to check on Caleb before returning to her day with Jason.

"Fifty ways to leave your lover. How many more were available to quit Sybil?"

Cheville turned and strolled out of the hotel.

The two women were seated at the bar, one pair from the tennis court. The other pair was nowhere to be seen, married, Sybil speculated. These two however were experienced competition. She recognized the species. But she had trump in the form of Caleb.

As they seated themselves on adjacent stools, the young bartender.

"I'm sorry ma'am but no minors are permitted to sit at the bar."

"I'm of age."

The bartender smiled. "I'm referring to the boy."

"My name is Caleb. What's yours?"

"Hailey."

"I'm his grandmother," Sybil lied. "His parents needed some private time," she continued.

Caleb regarded her quizzically.

Hailey nodded

"He is still a minor, a kid."

"I'm his guardian until they are," Sybil paused for effect, "Finished."

"It might be a while," Caleb said, knowing how much Cheville enjoyed shopping. He had seen Sybil pass money to her before she and Jason left the hotel.

Hailey stood there; mouth open.

"It might be a while," Sybil echoed, "or they might return in the next two minutes. I don't pry into private matters."

It was Caleb's turn to be speechless.

"As you can see, he's a mature minor. Are you new here, Hailey?"

"I'm filling in for Amy, the regular bartender. But she would tell you the same thing. Me, I've heard all types of stories, ma'am."

"It's Sybil, Hailey."

"People tell me all sorts of things, Sybil. But Caleb is still a kid."

"So he will drink milk."

It was clear that Sybil was not convincing Hailey.

"You are correct, Hailey. But then consider him a kid, a young goat."

Hailey's head tilted slightly to one side. That was a good sign, Sybil thought.

"Caleb is a young goat, and goats can be service animals. So consider Caleb my ADA protected service animal. They are permitted here in your inclusive bar. I can see the sign from here." Sybil was not sure if such a sign existed but told herself that it should.

"Is he potty trained?" Hailey joked, and Sybil knew that she had won the debate."

"I can assure you Hailey, that he is potty trained.

"Can you pour me a glass of cabernet and a.."

"A glass of milk for Caleb?" Hailey suggested.

"Chocolate, please," Caleb added.

The two enjoyed their respective drinks on what was a dry day for the three female customers in the bar, for Caleb was the only patron there of male persuasion.

CHAPTER TWENTY-FOUR

The following day, Cheville offered to take Caleb around town and to ride the train for as many circuits as she could tolerate.

After lunch, Sybil and her nephew were drinking iced coffee at the bar.

The bar top was long and narrow and dark. It stretched from the wall that separated diners from drinkers to the half dozen high tops that sat before the unlit fireplace. It was cozy, yet Sybil regretted that it was too warm to drink hot chocolate next to such a magnificent hearth.

Their conversation was heated in the odd way that cold can be hot.

Overhead, the ceiling was laid in a consistent gray tin pattern that seemed to refract the emotion.

"Do what you want in life Jason. Being happy is best achieved by ignoring the vast majority of your fellow human beings."

"I need more than happy."

Sybil had no response to that request, so she continued her previous thought.

"They aren't your fellows at all. Too much effort is wasted on trying to find the good ones. Its chasing rainbows."

"Like you are now?"

"I have my dreams, you have yours."

"On that we agree. But.."

"These folks commemorate this person's dream or this person's vision. Those persons are dead. I don't worry about their dreams. We all have dreams. They're dead. As for their dreams, dead men don't tell tales, and they don't dream. Hell, that's one of the perks of being dead. Or so it's said."

"I pity you, Aunt Sybil."

"I have no desire to review your list of my deficiencies. What would be the point?"

"To change?"

"I am not willing to change who I am because you don't like it. It's easier for me to replace you in my life than for me to replace me in yours."

"If you,"

Their conversation was cut short by the arrival of corvette man and a young woman. The couple sat a polite distance away and, noticing Sybil's and Jason's drinks, ordered the same.

"Who are they?" Sybil asked the bartender, indicating with a nod of her head, the man with the corvette, 'Not dead yet' and the young woman beside him.

"She's young enough to be her daughter," Sybil added, just an untimely quiet fell in the bar.

The bartender's head swiveled to regard the pairs of age mismatched couples, her long ponytail flicking back and forth, with Jason glancing in rhythm at her withers on each far turn.

"You should switch," she suggested, her experience risking her tip.

"Oh, did I say that aloud," she added, hedging her bet.

196

"She is that young indeed," the man said directly to Sybil.

"And the young man," he began.

"He's my nephew," Sybil stammered.

"I'm sure," he said, then paused dramatically, "pleased to make your acquaintance. My name is Victor Hampton, and this young lady, young enough to be my daughter, is in fact my daughter, Doctor Lauren Hampton."

"I'm Sybil and this is my nephew," Sybil said, blushing despite herself, "Jason."

"No last names?"

"Not on a first date," she replied, pleased that her aggressive move into humor resulted in Victor blushing.

He was a quick study and responded easily.

"Are you driving the white hearse?"

"Yes," admitted Jason sheepishly.

Sybil did not let the insult to her treasure go unreciprocated.

"Yours fits like a coffin."

"I'm not dead yet."

He dressed as an older but not quite an old man. He retained a vestige of male vanity, an aphrodisiac to many women. He cared what others thought of him, or, Sybil reasoned, he cared what his daughter perceived strangers thought of him. Sybil studied him slowly. He dressed well, matching adequately the current fashion styling, clean, pressed, appropriate for the venue.

Sybil was glad that she had brought her complete set of perfumes. She had the perfect one for her Victor mood. Lauren would have concurred with having the correct scent for the occasion.

"I noticed the handicapped parking sticker. I'll likely get one if I become infirm also."

Victor laughed at the insult.

"It's for the car, not me."

Jason raised his eyebrows.

"It requires better parking places. They are wider and offer less chance of an inadvertent ding."

There was a moment of silence.

"I picked up some medical jargon from Lauren, for good measure."

"You're complicit in this?" Jason asked, Sybil taken aback at her nephew's flirting.

The father answered

"Complicit? It's a parking place, not insider trading. I don't take the last spot either. As far as Lauren, she is not aware that she's helping me."

"I was going to compliment her on helping you. It is not malpractice."

Sybil was perturbed at the distraction her nephew was causing and was gratified to see Cheville and Caleb appear.

"The train was fine, but we're done now," Cheville said, then noticed the other patrons. Introductions were made, but they were as before, first names only. No relationships, real or fabricated were provided. The Hampton's were not family, neither genuine nor Deiters.

Soon, only Sybil and Victor remained in the bar from the two families that had met by accident.

"The boy looks like a fantastic kid."

"He is. But too soon he will be a teenager. I worry about teenagers. They can get into so much trouble."

Victor nodded somberly.

"I can buy heroin easier than getting Caleb vaccinated. Kids overdose all the time. Nowadays its expected. Overdose," she snorted.

"As if teenagers have PHDs in chemistry or pharmacology and accidently miswrote a prescription."

"Are those the parents?"

"She is. He's..... he's whatever."

"So, he's not the father? The boy could have done worse," the bartender, Amy, wryly commented, alert to this unanticipated alteration in Jason's status.

"He's a hunk. Lauren thinks so too, I bet."

Sybil reappraised her nephew, then returned her attention to Amy.

"You might need glasses, Amy my dear."

She shrugged.

"Usually, I'm further ahead not seeing too clearly in this job."

"What are their plans?" Victor asked Sybil.

"Ask them yourself."

"They don't include you?"

"Mine don't include them."

"Oh."

She saw the surprise on his face.

"Don't shoot the messenger."

"I would not consider it."

"They don't strike me as well matched. I never met her until this trip began. She does not resemble the girl that I thought he was dating."

"How would you know if you never met her?"

"Not physically. He showed me a picture of her once, it's the same person."

"How then?"

"Jason, it's hard to describe. He likes to write, poetry for example. He sent me a sample once, maybe hoping I could offer input. I used to be a teacher.

I remember one phrase of his:

'He speaks in love, she in dollars. They're short of both'."

"I like it."

"They pack lightly."

"That's a positive."

"They live lightly."

"That's a negative. Or a positive. I don't know."

"I did not raise Jason. I'm not Santa or Mrs. Claus."

"I'd ask your opinion, but it's written on your face."

Victor grinned.

"What about his girlfriend, Cheville is it?"

"Yes, Cheville. As I said, she is not the person that I expected. She's a woman."

"So are you."

"Thanks for noticing, Victor."

"Women don't do anything without a plan. If we are leaving the farm, we have another horse saddled and stashed behind the barn, ready to go."

He chuckled at her honesty.

"Very true," he said.

"Honesty is my vice. I've weighed having it excised but decided against it."

"Truth deteriorates into lies and lies can age well, morphing into verity. It becomes not a question of which is which, but which is when.".

"Which explains why there are no clocks in Heaven."

"I thought that no one else had noticed."

"How does the story end?"

"We are in a story?" Sybil flirted.

"You might say that. Life is a story. That makes it worth living.

"Don't you think so, Amy?" he asked the bartender who was passing by.

The bartender nodded.

"And good food, and sleep, and" Sybil left the sentence unfinished but understood.

"Look in the mirror," he commanded, pointing to the long glass that adorned the wall behind the bar and extending its length.

"Tell me what you see."

"Okay. Well, I see you and me, and some of the other patrons. None of them as well dressed as us. None of the ghosts that a hotel as old as this must have. Give me a hint."

"You don't need one. You spotted them immediately."

"I did? Fantastic. Who or what are the them that I identified?"

"It takes one to know one."

"What? Oh, the ghosts that I didn't see. So now I am one of them? A ghost? I was hoping that I had more time to finish things. No matter."

Sybil quickly finished her wine.

"That was good. Not a ghost of sweetness. Does this mean that drinks are free as of now?"

She answered her own question by ordering another glass of cabernet. If I am a ghost too, this might make for a fun afterlife."

"We are both ghosts."

"I gathered that. Still, you're required to pick up the tab."

He smiled and nodded.

"Of course."

"We see one another, but the others."

"Ooohh," Sybil exclaimed.

"I'm referring to the young,"

"I've a lifetime membership to that club. Honorary at this point, I confess."

"They don't see us the same way as other people of their generation. We are.."

"Invisible?"

He shrugged.

"But we are not invisible to each other. Australians can't see Polaris, and I've never glimpsed the Southern Cross, but they exist. They are important."

"That's not what I mean."

"I will tell you what you mean. What you should mean. I'm very good at it."

He laughed despite himself and her certitude.

"We are both glowing, incandescent in one another's eyes. Two flickering bulbs, still hot to the touch. No LEDs for us."

"Yes, that is what I meant," abandoning his now forgotten argument.

"Two white hot embers," he continued.

"Tell me more. This I like."

"Fading, but.."

"You could have dropped that part. I'm going to pretend you didn't say that.

"Ok," he replied.

"Incandescent. Period."

"Two ghosts connecting across the reflection of a barroom looking glass. I've been served better pickup lines, but not recently. It will do."

Sybil finished her wine.

"I'm ready."

"For what?"

"Incandescence."

Victor reached into his inside jacket pocket and retrieved his wallet. He opened his wallet to extract money for the drinks and a photograph fell out of it onto the bar. It was of a woman.

"My late wife," he explained.

"Two years last month," he said in response to the unasked question.

"Lauren stayed with me for a while, then she bought me a dog. Then she convinced me to buy the car that you ridicule."

"It's a pretty car."

"That was my motivation for purchasing it. I had always wanted a pretty car."

They laughed together. Well.

"Then Lauren moved out, taking the dog with her. She told me a few weeks ago that she took the dog, Lacy, to the animal shelter.

Not to dispose of it," he said quickly in answer to Sybil's questioning look, "but to have Lacy's input in selecting their new companion. Lacy would spend more time with the new arrival than

Lauren would, her entire remaining life more likely than not.

So Sybil, I know about the planning abilities of women."

He replaced the photograph carefully back in his wallet.

"Let's talk more in the morning, we can meet here or at the restaurant a few blocks away. Or the coffee shop across the street."

"I'd enjoy that," Sybil said pleasantly, and watched Victor walk to the stairs leading up to his room."

She took another sip of her wine and sighed. It was nearly time for her to retire as well. As she was preparing to stand, Cheville arrived, trailed by Caleb.

"He sure does follow you around."

"Like a golden lamb," she joked.

"He has a guilty look."

"Guilty of what?"

"I don't know what exactly. But I've seen it scores of times on the faces of my male students."

"Perhaps he is tired. I saw Victor going upstairs. He seems nice. His daughter, too."

"He carries a photo of his dead wife in his wallet. An old photo I might add. She died two years ago. Last month, so that makes it bit longer."

"A month longer."

"A man who does that is not ready for an unserious relationship. He's still stuck in a serious one with a ghost."

"Did you stop to consider that you might be the unsophisticated libertine."

"That's a big word."

"I had to look it up," Cheville said, smiling.

"What do you mean?"

"The photo might have meant that he was open only to nsa."

"NSA?"

"No strings attached," a juvenile voice provided.

"Doesn't anyone read?" it added.

"Are you truly looking for a relationship with him. You've known him a matter of hours."

"If you use the word relationship when discussing your relationship, you have no relationship."

"And what does that mean?"

"It means that I am tired."

"Not guilty?" Cheville asked in an attempt to cheer them both up.

"Not guilty. Not tonight."

CHAPTER TWENTY-FIVE

Lauren was seated with Cheville, Jason, and Caleb for breakfast. She was nervously awaiting the arrival of her father. It was awkward being with Jason in this pseudo family setting.

Through one of the hotel windows, she saw a man walking his dog. For a moment she thought that it was his father, but no, that wasn't him. Even the dog was a different color.

It was the slow pace that was the same. Men walk with their dogs, slowly, enjoying the time together. Women see it as exercise, anxious to complete it. Just the reverse when it comes to a stroller.

She was beginning to make her excuses when she saw Sybil and Victor enter the hotel through the front door.

They made their way to the table at a relaxed gate and seated themselves in the two open chairs.

"We already had breakfast," Sybil said.

"Outside," she added, winking at Cheville.

"It's one of the perks at being our age. Rising early is a choice, not a work requirement," said Victor.

"Please, go ahead and order."

As they awaited their meals, Victor began speaking.

"I used to think that children and cats were the best problem solvers."

"Cats and kids?" asked Jason.

"They both have limited responsibilities and plenty of time. Nevertheless, they eventually come up with a solution."

"I'm not sure that I agree with your logic."

"Then you won't like my new theory."

Jason laughed.

"Go ahead, I'm all ears."

"I've added retirees to the list. We have reduced career pressure, and more time to think. As a method of testing this, Sybil and I have decided to take a few days off."

"A few days off from a road trip?" Cheville asked amusedly.

"And take a drive somewhere. We will return in two days."

"What about our tennis rematch?" Caleb asked practically.

"We can reschedule for after our return."

"I have a better idea," Victor said.

Lauren would not have been surprised if her father had added 'honey'.

"Lauren can fill in for you."

"If you are leaving dad," Lauren began.

"That is a wonderful suggestion, Victor," Cheville said quickly.

"I'd enjoy your company, Lauren. We all would," she added pleasantly.

Lauren blushed at the last few words," yet she could detect no sarcasm either in Cheville's tone of voice or in her facial expression.

"The room is paid for dear. So is it settled?"

Victor looked around for confirmation. Receiving nods from all of the diners, he said simply,

"Excellent. Have a good breakfast. We will see you in two days."

Victor and Sybil stood quickly and turned to leave.

"Like newlyweds," reflected Lauren.

"You're leaving now this very minute?" Lauren demanded.

"Yep."

"We are already packed," added Sybil.

The couple hurried away before any objections could be raised.

"I've been stood up by my own father," Lauren thought.

Later, Jason and Cheville spoke privately

"Call it what you will. This may be as you say, an extended joy ride for a terminally ill nymphomaniac."

"That would make a good film."

"Or something completely innocent."

"Sybil and completely innocent cannot be in the same sentence."

After a few hours, it was clear to all that while they had enjoyed having Victor and Sybil around, they could have as much fun without either present.

Lauren acquiesced and agreed to serve as the fourth in Caleb's championship.

"They are really poor players," Lauren told herself.

Fortunately, Caleb was more than willing to chase errant balls.

"Can we talk for a minute?" Cheville asked before they switched teams to boys versus girls.

"Sure," Lauren replied, and the pair headed to the ladies room.

"I need to tell you something," Cheville whispered to Lauren.

"People confide in strangers and doctors. So I'm double trustworthy," Lauren replied, a smile masking trepidation

Jason noticed that the rest was taking longer than normal.

"Strategy" he said to Caleb.

"PITA girl talk," Caleb mocked.

"Adults are so unhappy and here I thought us kids were whiners. If seventy more years of whining is what I have to look forward to, what's the point of growing up? I'd be better off dead, or simply remaining a kid. That's it, I will stay as I am.

Life as an adult is too long. Why do you do it?" he asked.

"Why indeed?" Jason asked distractedly.

"Aunt Sybil is lucky in a way. She doesn't have much longer to complain."

"You're taking over for her."

"I'm the one who is friggin' screwed."

"Where did you learn that word?" Cheville exclaimed, as she and Lauren returned.

"Friggin?

It's for polite company. It really means.."

But Cheville's hand covered his mouth.

"We know Caleb," she said.

The foursome resumed play, the break having been worthwhile for the women, as both their games improved, but then Lauren played well to begin with.

CHAPTER TWENTY SIX

"Cheville," Caleb began.

The young woman sighed. She recognized the tone of the boy's voice, the special way that he said her name. It was his own private, oral antiseptic that he administered before delivering whatever notion he had created.

She usually thought herself ready for Caleb's latest injection, but she was invariably wrong.

"We could stay here."

"You could take a job."

"What about school?"

"That won't start again for months, and besides, schools have to accept kids like me."

"Kids like you?"

"Yeah," he replied, seeing no need to explain what should be clear to Cheville. Adults had such a hard time with truth.

"They should fix the lie once," he thought, not for the first time.

"I'll think about it," Cheville answered. Caleb recognized it for the no that it was. Adults can be so confusing. They claim not to have time, but they waste so much of it on lies.

"Well, he had given Cheville the first pick," Caleb thought, deciding to speak with Aunt Sybil next. He would need to adjust his presentation to her. She was returning today. He would approach her then, or tomorrow.

The next day, when he had maneuvered a few moments alone with the older woman, he began his pitch.

"Cheville has had job offers."

"That's nice."

"I overhear her telling Jason nearly every evening."

"Eavesdropping is not polite," she said mildly. Both of them understood what she meant, don't get caught.

"Jason should find a job, too. With Cheville. He is able to work. He should work. I'm right."

"That can wait."

"Why?"

"Well, there are lots of jobs, and it would end the trip."

"For them."

Sybil focused all of her attention on the boy. She nodded slowly; a mixture of amazement spiced with fear on her face.

"What does that mean, Caleb?"

"We could continue together, just the two of us."

Sybil's concern gave way to amusement as the boy continued pitching his plan.

"I can drive. I am a quick leaner. All my teachers say that about me. You used to be a teacher. So you know that what I'm saying is true."

He paused for breath.

"I don't complain. We could share the same room..."

"Sybil covered her mouth with her left hand.

"I don't need much. I don't complain like... and we could stop whenever you want. And the

214

backroads are good for my driving. All I need is a cushion. Aunt Sybil, your suitcase would fit perfect.'

"Perfectly," she corrected automatically.

Caleb interpreted the grammar fix as agreement.

"If we get pulled over. We won't because I will drive very good, and there are no police cars on back roads. If we do, you can pretend to be sick, and they will let us go. Or lead us to a hospital. That would be fun."

Sybil wondered if Caleb had been speaking with Lauren's father, Victor. Two boys, separated by a half century or more.

"And I don't eat much."

"Oh yes you do, more as each day passes."

"We are a perfect match, Aunt Sybil," Caleb said, seriously.

"I doubt that."

A perfect match.

Sybil had heard those three words so many times, from so many men. Probabilities, implausibilitys, impossibilities. But never from a man as young as Caleb. Now she had three, Caleb, Victor, and Jason. Two were family, leaving only one a viability.

They were alone, and Sybil was a bit bored, she admitted to herself.

"We are? In what way?" she asked the boy.

"You're energetic, and fun, and cool."

"What about you?"

"His young face expressed shock that she had posed such a question."

"Me too," he said simply.

"You too what?"

215

Caleb frowned. Perhaps his aunt didn't really see him in the same manner that he thought of himself.

"I'm energetic, and fun, and..."

"And cool?" she interrupted; her voice full of the best doubt that she could muster.

"And cool," he said after a moment's hesitation.

"For nine," he added in response to her resistance.

"I'm not as cool as you. But you've had years' head start."

"What do we do with Jason and Cheville."

Caleb hesitated again.

"I know that he is your nephew, but he is in a ditch."

Sybil did not ask what the term meant; it was clearly not a vote of confidence.

"And Cheville?"

He shrugged. That was as decisive as consignment to a ditch.

"You could teach me. But not much, I am pretty cool."

"So, its settled."

"What is settled, Caleb?"

"We leave them here in Lebanon, or in the next town. You probably owe them something, you know, like a notice. They give Jason notice all the time."

"Jason needs time," Sybil said to herself.

To Caleb, Sybil responded jokingly,

"You might be able to teach Jason how to be cool, if you aren't able to learn from him."

"He and Cheville aren't working out. I'm not surprised,"

"Why aren't you surprised," Sybil asked, herself very surprised.

"She's not the mothering type, and that is what he needs."

"For you?"

"Cheville told me that 'Dreams are how we make life of sense.'"

"Dreams can be like that, I suppose."

"Are they the same for you?"

"Well," Sybil began. "How to answer the boy?" she wondered.

"The best dreams are for the waking hours, those that arrive during sleep are worse than useless. It matters not at all if one were nine or ninety."

"I had a stupid dream last night," Caleb replied.

"I had a horse, and he was hungry. So my horse was nibbling on loose strands of hay that lay here and there. He was nodding at the idea of my buying bales. I nodded as well," Caleb said, demonstrating his nod.

"This was the oddest part of the dream."

"What was?"

"That I was going to buy bales of hay. I had a wallet. And money. I was driving home with my horse and buggy. But we don't have a home to drive home to. And we don't have a place for a horse.

I wish that I could remember his name. A name would make him real. Or more real. I woke this morning, and I checked my pants for my wallet. But it wasn't there. It wasn't real either."

Sybil sat there, lost for words.

"And then I thought that I would talk to you. Cheville won't mind."

CHAPTER TWENTY-SEVEN

"He was a shorthaired, orange cat. I discovered soon that he was a mediocre cleaner.

But that made for two mediocre cleaners in the house, when only one was needed, and I had already filled the position."

"What did you do?"

"We worked it out." She did not expand on the meaning of work it out, but Jason seemed to vaguely recall such an animal, the few times that he had visited his aunt as a child.

"Cheville has elected to remain here."

"In Lebanon?"

Jason nodded.

"For how long?"

"For good. She finally accepted one of the job offers. I did not ask which one. It doesn't matter to me.

"And Caleb?"

"What about Caleb?"

"He will need to enroll in school and be attended to when Cheville is working. All of the items that need to be resolved before she begins work."

"Caleb is coming with us."

"I don't believe it. You can really pick them. I suppose you had to settle."

Jason said nothing, it was another insult to ignore.

"She is abandoning her own son."

"It's been done before."

"By Cheville? I wish I had known before."

"Before what?" Jason did not wait for her response.

"Besides, she is not Caleb's mother."

"I don't understand."

"My priorities do not revolve around ensuring that you understand all of the details of my personal life. We hardly know each other, Aunt Sybil."

"We are family, Jason."

"You picked a great time to acknowledge it."

"Cheville is not his mother? But she has been your girlfriend for years."

"Cheville is not my girlfriend. She never has been."

"Oh."

"Caleb's mother was Cheville's sister."

Sybil strained to remember, finally saying, "Cheryl."

"Yes, the one with the normal name," his voice free of bitterness.

"Does Caleb blame himself for her death?" Sybil asked herself.

"No," she decided.

The regret gene, while not bred out of the family line, skipped a generation.

"She died of an overdose of painkillers."

"Is her sister suing?"

"Cheville?"

"Who else? For Caleb's benefit. He has a future after all. The money would help."

"It always does. Isn't that your motto?"

"Don't try to change the subject. You can't slither away from the discomforts of life. You haven't answered my question."

"You haven't answered my question, he echoed."

"I don't have a motto. That's so new age."

"But you like money?"

"I like money, and apple pie, and a lot of other things in life. Your turn."

"Is Cheville suing?"

"Yes."

"No."

"Why not?"

"Who would she sue?"

"This is America. Ask an attorney that question."

Jason's lethargy annoyed her more today than normally.

"If Cheville can't or won't sue, then the responsibility falls to you. Yes, responsibility. You can't dodge this one."

"Who said I was?"

"So, you accept then? Fantastic."

"I didn't say that."

"He is your son, Jason."

"Is Caleb your son?" Sybil asked a moment later when Jason stood there silently.

"The attorney would ask you to take a DNA test. Don't worry, he would add that to the contingency bill, if you pass."

"And if I don t?"

Sybil wanted to slap her nephew, to strike him even more forcefully than she had that first time.

How long ago that seemed now? A different time in another world.

"You still have a case," she said, more confidently than she believed herself.

"Lack of companionship and consortium, something like that. The jurors love to reward that sort of complaint, especially Lifetime romance addicts."

"That describes Caleb's mother."

He paused then said,

"There is no case."

"The doctor, the nurse, the hospital's administration."

"What are you rambling on for?"

"For Caleb."

"I thought that you didn't like him."

"That doesn't matter."

"Nor does your imaginary case. Are you being obtuse to annoy me, or do you really not understand?"

Sybil frowned at the question. Jason took her scowl as the latter.

"The case is important to Cheville. She needs a reason, a reason to believe."

"Neither you nor she can live a 70 years long life modeled on a three minute song. No matter how attractive the lyrics or how talented the singer.

There is no reason to believe.

There was no doctor, no nurse, no hospital. She died at home."

"I see," Sybil answered, Jason knew that she did not.

"This is no time for secrets."

Jason smiled at his aunt's plea. He had used that exact phrase with her only days ago.

"Just between us," she uttered as apology.

"She was an addict. She died. In the bedroom. With a needle in her arm. It was fentanyl. Illegal fentanyl, drugs, opioids. Whatever word you understand."

"I see," Sybil whispered, and this time she did indeed see.

"The recommended dose for fentanyl is zero, so each of her doses was an overdose. It was inevitable, a play in which I was the male lead, but one in which no number of rehearsals prepared me for the ending. All I know that there was no grand finale, only a final curtain, and a dark room afterwards."

"I need to have a DNA test any way."

"Why?"

"Caleb still needs a father. And I'm handy."

"No, you are not handy. You just happen to be here. You would not be any woman's first choice, but since you are the only choice, it is"

"My responsibility."

"I'm happy to see that you are coming around."

"Who said I was? It doesn't matter, it's my choice alone."

"Now you're pro-choice?"

"Laws are meant to be twisted."

"Is that your motto?"

"It will do for now."

"Do you remember Lauren?"

"A last name would be helpful."

"Lauren Hampton, the daughter of your.."

"Yes, the doctor. What about her? If I remember correctly, and I do, you seemed to be interested in her. What she saw in you..."

"She wanted to keep an eye on you and her dad. I thought that I could use her."

"Of course you did."

"To get a free DNA test for me and Caleb."

"Oh," Sybil said as her way of apology.

"And what were the results."

"She wouldn't do it."

"Not at first."

"Eventually she did."

"I think it was just to prolong her contact with you, through her I mean."

"I'm his father."

"Congratulations."

"She ran additional tests."

"For genetic diseases?"

"Not exactly. I had to be sure. It would have been kinder if I had been disappointed sooner."

"People act so foolishly that I've concluded that its deliberate. Its performed expressly in order to emphasize their stupidity."

"Why?"

"I pondered that question for a long time. It must be for my benefit. There is no other explanation."

"Ok," Jason said, hoping that his briefest of responses would discourage her from continuing.

"Shakespeare was wrong: 'The whole world's a stage' and everyone a player."

"It sounds reasonable to me," Jason said, regretting that he had stepped into this game. She nearly always won, and the few times that she didn't she made his winning seem cruel.

"Except me."

"I'm the intended audience. It is a grand production, with me the sole royal spectator.

"Jason, you could have been a writer, or a poet."

"I tried. And I failed."

"Writing?"

"And poetry."

"There is no such thing as a failed poet."

"Really? I'm unique."

"Certainly. Poor poets? Yes. Unappreciated? Without doubt. Failed? Never."

"Aunt Sybil, I'll be blunt. Cheville is convinced that you are ill."

"I'm not ill."

"I knew it. This is such a relief."

"Cheville was, we were all worried. Cheville was convinced that you were sick.'

"I am sick.

Jason said nothing, shocked into silence.

"I'm so sorry, Sybil,' Cheville said.

"I sick of living,' Sybil said, then paused. It wasn't for effect but to find words to externalize what had only been internalized as feelings.

"Of living the way I have."

"All the men?"

"Oh no, that part is fine."

"All the complaints?"

"What complaints?"

"What then?"

"Just being in Brentville. It's a wonderful town, there is no place better."

"But there is more to see?"

"That is part of it. There are towns to visit, sights to see. Brentville will be there when I return."

"If I disappear, you can remember for both of us. If I die before I return, remember that I prefer a stone to a stove."

"You are not dead yet.

"I'm old fashioned that way."

"I remember the tombstones in Whitland. Each one had a few lines of poetry, a handful of words, and numbers. Why do we think that the numbers are more important than the words?"

"I don't," Cheville interjected.

"What would you have carved on your marker?"

"You don't?".

"Maybe, 'Let me out'."

EPILOGUE

Jason was still surprised to read Sybil's address on mail addressed to him. It had been over a month, and he supposed that in time the novelty would wear off. He had found a job, not just work, and Caleb was ecstatic having his own room.

The return address was blank, and the postmark was Nebraska. He knew no one in that state. Even the handwriting was unfamiliar, but as it was in cursive, and not printed, he guessed that it was from Sybil. She had called a few times, arranging to give him check signing authority on one of her checking accounts in her absence.

He and Caleb had settled into what was, if not a normal father/son relationship, the closest to it that either of them had known. What was this about to change?

Jason hesitated to open the envelope and decided to let it cure for a day or so.

Eventually, he convinced himself to slice open the paper missive with one of the many paring knives that decorated the kitchen. He sat alone at one of the stools at the marble covered island and extracted the contents from the envelope.

It was a birthday card. It perplexed the twenty-eight-year-old, as it was intended for a ten-year-old boy. He noticed that there was no signature.

Things had been going well, very well. Too well, apparently. The card was obviously meant as an insult. It was clear, in black and white, and blue and green, and a touch of orange, what she thought of him.

In case he had not received her unmistakable message, Sybil had added a slip of paper, folded inside the card.

"I guess Hallmark doesn't sell many, Happy Birthday Moron cards," Jason said aloud.

He unfolded the paper, which he considered as a malevolent fortune cookie.

"Jason,
I hope that you and Caleb are doing well and keeping the house clean. If you find the Odyssey too much for in town use, you have my permission to sell it. It's served its purpose, and it no longer brings me joy. Even if you do drive it, please sell it in any case. It's a good time to sell any vehicle so you should get a good price. By the way, Lauren says hello."

Yep, she still treats me as a ten-year-old, Jason thought. There was more and he forced himself to read it.

"I'm not sure when I will return. During our Trip," Jason noticed that she capitalized the word like some holy experience,
"You told me that you ran DNA tests to verify the relationship between you and Caleb. Knowing your deviousness, and I mean that as a compliment, I suspect that you ran more than one. I noticed a difference in your behavior soon after we

spoke that day. I do mean devious as a compliment, Jason. It can be a useful attribute at times.

I still have mixed emotions about this, not deviousness. About that, I'm certain."

Jason noticed that the writing was tinier with each succeeding sentence, as Sybil words approached the bottom of the single, small page.

"You'll notice that I left Caleb's card unsigned"

Jason read that line several times, his smile growing larger each time that he did so.

"I'll leave it to you to sign it. I hope that you can manage cursive."

At that, Jason laughed aloud.

"It's up to you to use either Aunt Sybil or Grandmother. Under no circumstances sign it Grandma."

Her own signature on the note read, in miniscule print,

"Love, Mother."